Dark Tides

A WICKED FAIRYTALE BOOK I

J.J. Marshall

Copyright ©2020 by J.J. Marshall

First Printing, 2020

ISBN: 978-1-7347724-0-1

Golden City
Alcovera
Aramore
Port
Adrella
Lowtown
Andover
Swallow Hallow
The Forest of Broken Souls

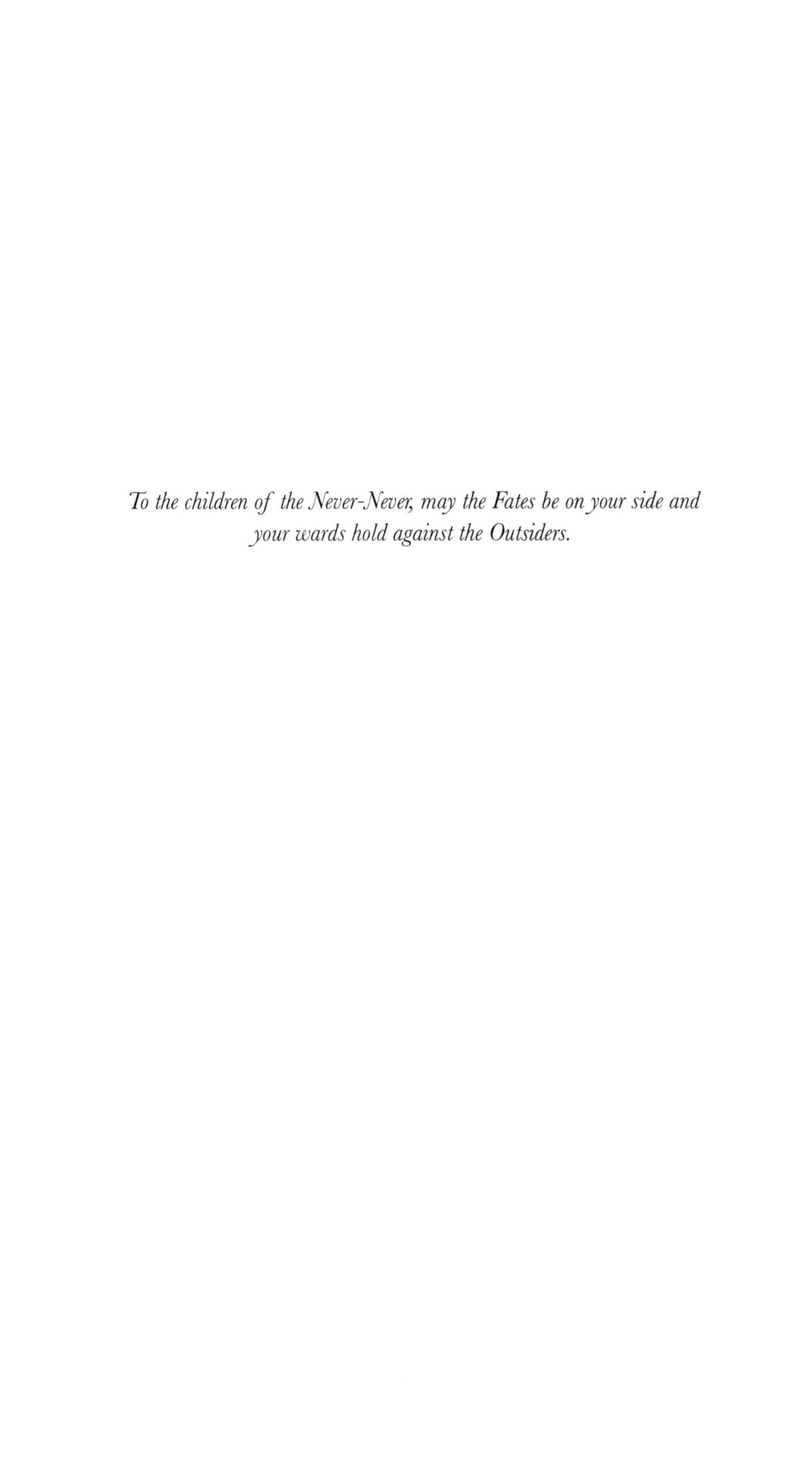

*To the children of the Never-Never, may the Fates be on your side and
your wards hold against the Outsiders.*

PART I

The water understands
Civilization well;
It wets my foot, but prettily,
It chills my life, but wittily,
It is not disconcerted,
It is not broken-hearted:
Well- used, it decketh joy,
Adorneth, doubleth joy:
Ill- used, it will destroy,
In perfect time and measure
With a face of golden pleasure
Elegantly destroy.
- "Water" by Ralph Waldo Emerson

PROLOGUE

*D*eep in the waters of the Adrellan Pass was a city made of crystal and inhabited by creatures of the sea. Adrella, as the metropolis was known, was ruled by a selfish king, labeled by most as the King of Sirens. The king wanted Adrella and all of the waters and land around it for himself, destroying anyone who sailed into the Pass above. He was determined to keep his kingdom and all of its treasures hidden and with good reason.

After his wife, the late queen, was brutally torn apart at the hands of Andoverian fishermen, the king grew dark and angry. His reign changed the course of the underwater city forever. His daughters became weapons against the land above, using their voices and songs to enchant sailors. They capsized ships and brought those intruders to a watery grave.

This pleased the king of the sirens, so much so, that he encouraged all of Adrella to utilize their gifts. Together, they would avenge the queen and destroy King Marlow of Andover and his kingdom.

But some of the sirens disagreed, wanting nothing

more than to live in peace. They fell in love with the men above and became pregnant, leaving their city and taking to land. Their bodies shattered as each siren underwent a transformation from sea to land, but their time in Andover was short, weakening their bodies day by day. When the time came for the sirens to give birth, the enchantment on their men wore thin, allowing them to see their children's true form. Large scales tore through flesh as they dotted the infant's arms and chest and serrated teeth appeared where teeth should not be. The offspring took on human form, changing only when immersed in water. The sailors called them monsters, but the siren women saw otherwise. Anger from rejection flowed through each siren woman, and taking vengeance for themselves and their children, the sirens ripped the flesh from the sailor's bones, devouring them whole before returning to the sea with their offspring.

King Marlow of Andover was furious, seeing his sailors murdered in his city and the streets running red with their blood. He called together the rest of his sailors and sent an armada of ships into the Pass to wage war on Adrella and avenge the lives that had been stolen from his kingdom. The water ran thick with blood and fearing the King of Sirens may win, King Marlow commissioned an enchanted crown for himself, one that protected the life of the wearer.

For many centuries the children of the sea fought against the children of the land, each trying to claim Adrella and seek revenge for themselves and each failing. War between sirens and sailors dwindled until eventually it was extinguished completely.

The King of Sirens grew weary of the humans and commanded his eldest daughter, Ophelia, to infiltrate the kingdom of Andover and gather information for him. Ophelia had no choice but to follow her father's orders.

She'd spent the better half of twelve months on land before returning with intel, but her body was weak and she inevitably perished. The king, struck by grief, buried his daughter and commanded the Adrellan troops to ready themselves for land and took to the world above himself. The sea and the land were ravaged by war once again until the King of Sirens perished. Adrella mourned the death of their king, and his second eldest daughter, Aramis, was chosen to ascend to his throne. She gratefully accepted, though her heart was tainted by darkness and she vowed to avenge her father. She would defeat the land and take the Adrellan Pass for Adrella.

ARAMIS

Queen Aramis sat upon her crystal throne, listening to the thrum of voices as sirens filtered into the throne room and took their seats among her court. Her grip tightened around her father's ancient golden trident as she thought quietly about her impending speech.

Her reign would bring change upon Adrella. It had to. The war raging between the sea and the land above had stolen too many lives, and the bloodshed needed to end. It was a decision Aramis had wrestled with for weeks.

"Your Highness," a friendly voice greeted from beside her. Shay, her best friend, was one of the most beautiful sirens in all of Adrella. She was as deadly as sirens came, and had been sought after by many suitors, but that was expected as she was the queen's advisor and closest confidant. Her long dark locks fell in waves past her neck, resting on her exposed sun-kissed breasts. Hints of purple and green on Shay's tail shimmered as the sun hit them. Shay ignored her glittering tail and lowered into her seat.

"You're so formal," the queen muttered, consumed in

her own thoughts as she turned her gaze away from her friend and towards her following. Aramis sucked in a deep breath before letting out a sigh. Gripping the armrests of her throne, Aramis rose. Those gathered fell silent, the men and women gazing upon their queen.

"For too long we have been at war. Sons and daughters of Poseidon dying brutal deaths at the hands of Zeus's kin. My heart breaks for our dead. They did not deserve to die. My father, your righteous king, did not deserve to die. My eldest sister, your first princess, did not deserve her fatal end." Aramis's voice rose, demanding to be heard.

"For as long as I can remember, there has been blood-shed. Our waters are painted red, our hands are stained in blood. I say, no more! We can coexist with the humans and allow them to pass through our waters without harm." Murmurs sounded throughout the room as the sirens shot wary glances towards their queen. Aramis set her jaw. She would be *damned* if her kingdom challenged her word. She raised her palm towards the crowd, quieting them. "I am not saying humans can be trusted and I'm not asking for you to trust them. I am; however, asking you to think of our fallen. Each and every one of you has lost someone dear to you in the war. I will not turn a blind eye to our loss. We will mourn and honor them the best way we can and end these senseless, brutal deaths.

"Living amongst the humans will grant us peace and prosperity. Adrella will flourish as will Andover, but it will take time. And in that time, Adrella will need eyes and ears above. Some of you have been selected to be just that—my eyes and ears."

"You're asking us to become nymphs for God's sake!" one siren shouted. Murmurs of agreement began to sound throughout the room. They were not freshwater nymphs, and to be asked to take to the land was offensive.

Aramis shifted under their gaze, her attention focusing on one young male. His eyes scrutinized the young queen and his fists were clenched at his side. Aramis blinked as she listened to the muttering of the room. Shay, to her right, arose. Aramis shifted her attention to her confidant, watching as her own fists clenched.

"You will watch your tongue when you speak to the queen, or I will carve it out myself and shove it down your throat as an example to anyone who dares to challenge her. Now, sit down and silence your mouth," Shay hissed, glaring into the tanned boy's sea-green eyes. Aramis watched silently as he moved closer to Shay, baring his teeth.

"You speak bold words in our queen's name, and yet you don't fear the same fate. You live your life in the lavish company of Our Majesty, while the rest of us stand the chance of being sent to the land. Have you ever endured the *Ascension*? Have you ever felt the burning of your tail as it splits into two? Have you ever felt the fire boil your skin as you push into the human state? No? How fortunate for you. Carve my tongue out if you like, but I for one, want to hear the queen's response." The court murmured again. Did they all disagree? Aramis held up her palm to the crowd. She turned to face the boy—no older than sixteen, a year younger than her younger sister—and pursed her lips. Serena would learn of her fate soon enough. Aramis blinked, taking in every detail of the boy. It wasn't often that a siren male was born into Adrella. His olive skin was etched with markings of battle, trophies of his victories both above and below the sea; his golden locks fell to his shoulders with ease. So young, and yet so hardened by circumstance. The boy remained unphased as Aramis approached him, ignoring Shay's objections.

"What is your name?" she asked, coming close enough

to touch the crowd, to touch the boy before her, and she did just that. Aramis reached out and gently tilted his chin back with her index finger. The boy's green-eyed gaze met with her own and then faltered.

"Tadd," he replied and swallowed. The queen watched his Adam's apple bob up and then down as his gaze flicked back to her own.

"Tadd," Aramis cooed, "we are far from naiads. It is true that every siren will have to endure the *Ascension*, but I have endured this, many times myself. I did not come to this meeting today on a mere whim and I certainly did not come unprepared."

"And you expect us to just follow you blindly?" Tadd sneered, speaking out of turn, yet again.

"Who do you think *you* are to question me, your queen?" Aramis asked. Irritation coursed through the young queen's veins as she stated, "I expect you to mind your tongue. Now, take a seat." She cleared her throat and fixed her eyes to her court.

"I have visited Andover and spoken to King Marlow myself. He has agreed to a peace treaty with our kind in return for a siren queen." Tadd crossed his broad, muscular arms and arched a brow at Aramis.

"We will *die* on the land. You are asking for us to willingly die for you. How is that any different?" he growled from his seat. Voices muttered their agreement throughout the court, as Aramis peered around. She had to get the court back under her control and avoid any further discussion on the matter.

"We may live shorter lives, but the bloodshed ends," she replied.

"And what of the siren queen, Your Majesty?" a smaller female asked, taking her place beside Tadd. Shay rose from her seat, catching Aramis's eye as the sun glinted off her tail.

"How dare you speak out of turn. How dare all of you speak out of turn!" Shay snarled. Aramis turned, gesturing for Shay to take a seat calmly, and returned her attention back towards the crowd.

"I'm glad you asked. The only way we can trust our kin will live in peace is to place siren royalty upon their throne. Andover will be ours."

"You plan to marry?" she heard Shay whisper behind her.

"Not me, but Serena," she replied over her shoulder.

"So, from this moment on, Princess Serena of Adrella is hereby betrothed to Prince Aaron Nolan of Andover. Long may she reign," Aramis said, her voice echoing through the room.

Voices roared as sirens stood from their seats. Even the queen's court shouted in outrage as she turned to sit back on her throne. She wasn't sure if her plan to destroy Andover would work, but Serena would destroy the humans from the inside out. Aramis sat tall and reached for her father's golden trident.

"My word is final," Aramis hissed, slamming the trident down upon the rocky floor beneath them. The throne room trembled, silencing the outrage of every siren. Aramis flexed her jaw, gritting her teeth together and took a deep breath before dismissing her court. She turned to face Shay, whose expression mirrored the grim feeling Aramis herself felt and whispered, "Gather Serena and bring her to me."

2

SERENA

The sun beat down on Serena as she rested on a sharply pointed rock above. The sun warmed her flesh as she stared up into the crystal blue sky. She didn't care about the speech Aramis had planned for the Kingdom. Her sister would fill her in later when she chastised her for being absent. Instead, Serena decided to wait for a ship to sail through the Pass, carrying her next victim. Seagulls squawked overhead, circling the waters in hope of a meal as Serena let out a groan. She, too, was hoping for a meal as her stomach grumbled, twisting and knotting in pain. It had been ages since she had tasted the flesh of a sailor, and with no ships in sight, it would be ages before she would taste another. She groaned again and flipped onto her stomach, staring at the shores ahead. Her stomach growled again when sounds coming from the shore caught her attention.

She focused her sights on a figure approaching the beach. He was handsome and looked divine.

"Okay belly," Serena whispered, patting her exposed milky stomach, "I'll get that human for us."

Slipping from the rock, the icy water enveloped Serena as she dipped below the surface. She followed the waves rolling onto shore, stopping close enough to keep her scales and fins hidden beneath the surface. The young man was beautiful, and Serena bet he would taste just as great. She approached silently, creeping in with the roll of the waves. His tanned skin poked through his white linen shirt, a size too large for him as it slipped from one shoulder and opened at his chest. She could faintly make out the hardened lines of his pecs. Serena licked her lips. His hair was darker than the darkest waters of the sea, and his eyes were blue and full of life.

A life she would take. A life she would watch slip from those bright eyes before she devoured them. Serena smiled at the thought and began to sing.

Come with me and then you'll see
For the children of the sea, we were born to be.
Die you must
To join us.
In our haunting melody.

Serena continued to sing, watching as the man's body stiffened. His gaze locked on her own as she repeated her melody, enchanting the boy to come to her, to slip beneath the surface and join her for eternity. He stood, transfixed on Serena and slowly moved into the water. Serena watched as his pants clung to him; her stomach grumbled again. She was close. So close.

Serena, she heard Shay's voice echo within her mind. Rolling her eyes, Serena continued to sing, watching as the boy grew closer to her. *Gods* was he divine. Only a few more steps before she would feast upon his flesh. Shay called through her mind once more, but Serena ignored her and reached for the boy's hand, feeling his icy touch. Then before she knew what had hit her, she was ripped beneath the waves, leaving the boy in her wake.

"WHAT DO YOU MEAN I'VE BEEN *BETROTHED*?" SERENA roared at Queen Aramis in her private quarters. Her blood boiled beneath her thick skin. "How could you do this to me? How could you sink so low as to sell me to the land king? I am the daughter of Poseidon! Gods! Do you ever think about anyone besides yourself? How could you be so selfish, Aramis?" Serena clutched at her skull, grazing her scalp with the points of her nails as she raked her fingers through her scarlet locks. She huffed a ragged breath and turned to face her sister.

Aramis lounged atop of a seaweed- covered rock she called a bed and watched the spectacle of her sister play out before her. Serena turned, gazing into her eyes with hate, picking at wounds she knew had yet to heal.

"Everything I do is for the kingdom," Aramis growled. "I remember what you did to Calix," Aramis said, changing the subject. Serena's body grew stiff, the name of the dead body hanging within the air. A ghost. A death that had occurred because of her.

"Poor, poor Calix. He never stood a chance, did he?" Serena remembered that day, remembered him dying on the beaches above. She could hear her sister's words.

"PUT HIM DOWN. LET HIS SECRETS DIE WITH HIM INSTEAD OF getting into Marlow's hands!" The princess shook her head, trying desperately to clear the memory from her mind. But she remembered that day vividly.

"I know a secret," Calix whispered, cupping Serena's face as he moved in closer. Their short romance had stirred something within the princess. She wanted Calix, forever and always. Serena smiled and leaned in, grazing Calix's lower lip with her own. Just a kiss, short and sweet, lit a fire within her belly.

"What sort of secret?" she asked.

"I know who the heir is." Serena smiled. So, did she. Pressing her lips in Calix's she let his mouth consume her thoughts. The murky water around them stirred. Something wasn't right. Serena looked around. Her senses pushed into overdrive. It was quiet. Too quiet for comfort.

"Hush up," she said to Calix, who was whispering sweet nothings into her ear. Shadows overhead sucked the light from the water around them, casting Serena and Calix into a black abyss. But Calix ignored Serena. Leaning in, he pressed his lips against the underside of her jaw.

"Cal," she whispered, every nerve in her body screamed. "Stop." Calix continued his onslaught of kisses, trailing them from her jaw down Serena's neck. The shadows overhead moved, as did Serena. Her hands pushed against Calix's olive-skinned chest. His hard muscles tensed under her touch, forcing him backwards as the water above them broke. A mess of knots and rope fell from above. Nets. Calix shouted, tangled within the heap. Screams tore from his throat, and his eyes grew wide with fear. Sailors. Andoverian sailors.

"Don't let them take me, Serena!" he shouted, twisting in the ropes. Serena tried to move, but something held her in place.

"Stay put," Aramis's stern voice whispered.

"I need to help him! Please, Aramis."

"No, Serena. Put him down. Let his secrets die with him instead of getting into Marlow's hands!" Aramis snarled from behind her.

"I can't. Please, Aramis. I love him," Serena cried.

"You're sixteen, Serena. You know nothing of love. Do it for Adrella. Secrets must stay within the family. Kill him or I will." Serena felt the pressure of her sister's grip slacken. She couldn't do *this. She just couldn't. But what other choice was there? To kill Calix with mercy or let him die by another's hand? She had to do it. Mercy was the only way. Taking their father's trident, Serena poised it above Calix's heart.*

"I love you. Forever and always, I'm sorry," she said, before plunging the trident into Calix's chest.

"You forced my hand," Serena snarled. "His blood is on yours!"

Aramis laughed. "If memory serves me right, his *blood,* foam, whatever you want to call it, was on your hands, Sister. Now, how do you think the kingdom would feel if they knew their princess was a cold-blooded murderer?"

"You selfish bitch!" Serena hissed. "You're really going to blackmail me? I was following your orders. We both know you can't share the throne." Aramis's lips perked into a sly grin as she swam closer to her sister.

"You will do my bidding or I will tell the kingdom what you truly are. A monster. Who do you think they will believe? Me, their just and righteous queen? Or the unruly, rebellious princess with a history of violence? I'm going with the first. You will marry Aaron Nolan Andover. You will be my eyes above the sea and when the time is right, you will murder both him and his father." Aramis stared only inches from her sister's face, feeling the heat radiate from the siren assassin.

"I hope you rot," Serena seethed. "I hope you rot in the darkest corners of the Pass for this."

"Hope is for the lonely and will only get you killed," Aramis said, her tone neutral as she studied her sister's raging features.

"I will die above the sea," Serena hissed back.

"You will live and you will succeed, for Adrella."

"How will I eat? I can't go around Andover killing mortals for sustenance!"

"Figure it out, Serena."

"Ophelia would have your tongue if she knew how you treat me," Serena snarled.

"Ophelia is dead!" Serena met Aramis's gaze. If she could kill the queen, she would have at that moment. Aramis's order rang through her body, crippling her. The siren queen's word was final. Serena closed her eyes. It would be no use to fight the order and endure the pain it entailed. So instead, she submitted, bowing her head as she stared deeply into the ground.

"When do I leave?" she asked, her voice low and even. She swallowed the lump that had formed in her throat and waited for her sister's response. She would kill the king because she had to. Then, she would kill and eat every person in the land above and return to the sea. She would bring the heir, and Adrella would be hers to do as she pleased. Of course, that left the matter of Aramis's death to be determined. And she *would* die.

"Tomorrow," Aramis replied. Serena bit into her lip, fighting the anger now flowing freely from her. She could kill Aramis for this. Tomorrow was too soon. She wouldn't have nearly enough time to get her affairs in order or say her goodbyes to those she cared for, not that there was really anyone left. Serena flicked her eyes to her sister, watching her fingers dance one after the other onto the rock. Aramis awaited a reply.

"I really have no choice in the matter so…" her voice trailed off. Serena did not want to do this. She just wanted to lounge on her rock above and eat sailors. How was that so bad? If she had to leave for Andover in the morning and undergo the change, then she needed to eat human flesh, now.

"May I be dismissed?" Serena gritted out, clenching her jaw together as her hands balled, and her nails dug into her palms.

"I suppose," Aramis replied nonchalantly, lifting her fingers to inspect her nails. "I've grown bored with your presence." Serena's nails dug deeper into her palms, threatening to slice her flesh open. She forced a smile to her lips and bowed her head.

"Yes, Your Grace." Serena headed back to the surface to lure another land dweller into her grumbling belly with her enchanting song.

3

AARON

*A*aron Nolan Andover sat in the crow's nest of his ship the *Camilla Delarose*, looking out into the ocean's blue waves. He was beyond furious when he found out he would have to marry a creature of the sea and nearly broke his crown as he removed it from his head, whipping it at the king. His blood boiled in his veins at the very thought of being with a siren. Aaron was never one for settling down, sailing from port to port. He loved the open waters and the freedom that came with it. Now he would have to settle down, take a bride and bear his father an heir to the throne. He wanted to *vomit*. To reproduce with a child of the sea would bring nothing but doom down upon their kingdom, and Aaron couldn't understand why his father would agree to such a thing.

"You will fetch Princess Serena and bring her back at once," King Marlow commanded, as he paced the dais before his throne. Candle-light flickered from the banquet tables, and the sounds of the servants' feet pitter-pattering about the room echoed through the air. Aaron gnashed his teeth together, ignoring the pain radiating up his jaw and stared at his father. His fingers curled into fists, fighting to contain the

electricity of the magic that was building. "We will hold a feast in your honor," the king continued, "and announce your engagement to the kingdom. The land and the sea will unite under one roof and our treaty of peace with Adrella will come to pass."

Treaty of Peace. The words rang through Aaron's mind. No more bloodshed, no more death, no more sailing with his crew and commanding his father's armada. No more freedom.

"But father—" he started to protest, but King Marlow held up a hand to silence his son. His word was final, and that's how Aaron had wound up on his last voyage.

He sighed, taking in the hefty scent of salt and ocean spray one last time while his crew sailed towards the infamous Adrellan Pass. Sweat beaded the young prince's brow as the midday sun beat down on him, soaking his trousers and shirt thoroughly. He relished the soft breeze that rustled his dark brown locks, flowing his cotton shirt in the wind and cooling his body. To the dismay of his father, Aaron was dressed for comfort. Cupping his hands around his eyes, Aaron blocked the sun from blinding him and took in the sight of the Pass. They'd spent a day's journey at sea—not long enough in Aaron's opinion—before reaching their destination.

Rocks lined the sides of the Pass, sticking out in sharp and jagged pieces. It was no wonder this place wrecked so many ships in his father's armada. His eyes flitted to the rock-shaped arch that stood at the entrance of the Pass and scampered into an upright position, slipping on the dampened wicker of the crow's nest. He outstretched a hand, catching himself on the mast and cursed under his breath at the splinters that bit into his palm.

"Ahoy! Petar!" he shouted, watching as the crew below grew still, their necks craning in his direction until the captain had called back.

"Ye called fer me?"

"Stop the ship," Aaron called out. "We'll wait for the fish bitch to surface. Don't venture forward."

"Then ye best keep yer eyes on the horizon, me prince," the captain called back. Aaron nodded and leaned his back against the mast, feeling the warmth of the day's sun pull from the wood into his body. He pulled a thin telescope from his black trouser pocket and fashioned the eyepiece against his right eye, and then he waited.

NIGHTFALL DESCENDED UPON THE ADRELLAN PASS, CASTING sheets of darkness over Aaron's ship. Aaron shivered and rubbed his arms with his hands, hoping to bring them some warmth. His teeth chattered as the air around him grew colder. He huffed a breath, watching the tendrils dance before his eyes and disappear. It had been a while since he'd been this cold, and although he knew he should have been dressed in heavier garb, Aaron had miscalculated and now suffered the consequences.

The captain of the ship, Petar, had offered him relief, but the young prince refused. If the siren surfaced tonight, then he wanted to be the one to call for her capture. Silence hung in the pass and down below. He could hear the crew snoring and the creak of the ship's boards every now and then. Aaron rubbed at his face, pushing the beckoning sleep away, and found his mind wandering as he looked into the vast darkness.

He wondered if the siren would put up a fight. Hell, he hoped she did. A smile played on his lips as he imagined pushing the blade of his dagger to her neck. He wanted to make her pay. Pay for the lives her kind had stolen from his crew. He wanted her to pay for the friends he'd lost. He wanted her to suffer the way he had suffered and mourned.

Treaty of Peace, those damn words rang through his brain again. Treaty, his arse. Aaron's jaw clenched, his teeth grinding over one another as the familiar pain ran up his jaw. He flicked his tongue over the edge of his front teeth and continued to glare into the distance.

If Serena came to Andover in pieces, the treaty would be void and the war his father had worked so hard to end, would all be for nothing. But Aaron liked the war. It took his father's attention off of him. Aaron rubbed at his face again and stifled a yawn. He knew he needed to fight sleep, push it off until daybreak, but the longer he leaned against the beam, the heavier his body grew. His eyelids grew heavy and sleep beckoned to him. Aaron yawned again and pushed his legs out, sliding his back down the rail. Although he hated to admit defeat, Aaron shut his eyes and welcomed the dark, allowing a dreamless slumber to possess him.

"Ahoy! Prince Andover!" Petar boomed from below. Aaron jolted awake, the sun baking his exposed skin. He winced as he shifted in the crow's nest and rubbed the sand from his eyes. Pain shot through his stiff limbs and back as he rose to his feet and looked below.

"Ay, Petar," he croaked. The captain, a man of nineteen, a year older than the prince, stared up at him. His eyes were dark brown, and he wore his hair chopped above his ears. His locks were sunbathed with streaks of gold and bronze, and his ears were rimmed with the finest gold earrings the kingdom had. He wore a white linen shirt, far too big for him that tucked into his worn tanned trousers.

He had weathered leather boots that sat just below his knees, and a sword buckled to his waist.

"Come down 'ere would ya!" he called. "One of me deckhands caught sight of a sea lass over yonder! Methinks she would be the bounty you seek!" Excited, Aaron fumbled for his telescope, searching the waters until he glimpsed the shine of a fin dipping beneath the waves. He continued to watch, hoping the creature would pop back above the surface, and grinned when he spotted her hoisting herself onto one of the jagged rocks. Her hair was dark red, darker than the finest rubies his father owned—the very ones that crested his crown back home—and her skin was milky and pale. Scales of seafoam green crested her arms, shimmering and turning iridescent in the sun's rays. Albeit she was a monster, but she was the prettiest damn monster he'd ever seen.

"Petar!" Aaron called from the nest, his mouth growing dryer the longer he stared at the girl. "Have the crew ready a boat. I'm going to get closer."

"Nay, I cannot allow ya to do that, me liege. Your safety is me greatest concern." Aaron sucked in a breath and fumbled for his canteen as his mouth continued to grow drier. He unclasped the lid and tipped back his head, emptying the contents of the canteen into his mouth. Water soaked his tongue, warm and tasting of old ale, but Aaron didn't care. He swallowed it down and tossed the canteen to the floor of the nest.

"I said get a boat ready for me. You dare question me?" he hissed back to the captain.

"Does Your Highness see a crown upon the lass's head?" Petar called back from the deck below. Aaron paused, his body growing rigid as he tore his attention back to the siren. No crown crested her brow, but he didn't care. He would find out who she was, one way or another. He smiled as his fingers grazed the hilt of his dagger buckled at his side.

"Does not matter," he called back. "I want a boat. Ready one for me at once or I will throw myself into the depths below and take my chances swimming!"

"You have a death wish if you seek to leave the ship," Petar replied before turning away from the prince. Aaron heard his comrade command a deckhand to ready a boat for him and grinned. He would figure out if this was the siren he was to capture and regardless of if she was or wasn't, things were finally getting interesting.

Aaron climbed down from his spot on the makeshift ladder and landed with a thud as his boots hit the deck. He checked his belt and pulled his dagger from its holster as his other hand plunged into his pocket and retrieved a vial with green contents. He knelt down, placing the dagger upon the deck and emptied the vial onto the blade. He watched the enchanted liquid soak into the dark metal until the blade no longer looked wet and carefully secured it back into his holster.

"Yer sure about 'dis?" Petar asked, clambering up to his side.

"Ay. About as sure as I can be," Aaron replied, pushing to his feet. He capped the vial and placed it into his best friend's hand.

"Silver don't contain beasts of the sea," Petar remarked, "but beasts of the night."

"Regardless, if the bitch attacks, perhaps the poison will slow her from turning to foam and returning to the sea."

Aaron outstretched his hand to his friend and watched as his friend gripped his forearm. "May the gods be with ya."

"If I should falter, you leave," Aaron commanded. He

and only he would die for the wretch. If he miscalculated, if the poison didn't hold, he would die and protect his crew.

"Ay," Petar replied before releasing Aaron. The prince sucked in a deep breath and climbed into the boat the crew had readied. It was now or never. Aaron watched as the crew lowered his boat into the calm sea below. The boat rocked with the waves as he clasped the oars in his hands and began to row.

Death wish or not, he would have his bounty bride.

4

SERENA

The sun felt like heaven against Serena's skin as she laid back against her rock. The air nipped at her skin in a familiar way and the waves whispered to her. Her body eased against the warmth of the rocks and she was at peace. She would miss this. She would miss Adrella and calling to sailors. She would miss being free. Serena let out a sigh and watched seagulls flying in circles above her in the baby blue sky.

Seagulls squawking and the hiss of water against rock, filled her ears until the crash of something hollow hit the sea. Serena sat up. She knew that sound all too well and scanned the surrounding Pass. She couldn't see the boat, but the scent of man in the air wafted through her nostrils. Fear and something else she couldn't place tickled her senses. She continued to survey the area, watching as the groan of wood on waves approached her. A boat, small enough to capsize if the wind was just right, crept around the sharp rocks of the Pass, its oars slicing through the waves. Serena's eyes narrowed, honing in on the vessel.

A boy, no older than eighteen at best, rowed closer to

her. His hair was shaggy and dark, ruffling in the breeze that carried salt and sweat to Serena's keen nose. She licked her lips as she watched his chest heave up and down with each push. He would be a tasty last meal and his stupidity would play in her favor.

Slipping from her place on the rock, Serena dipped back into the icy waters, feeling the familiar prick of the sea. She crept along the boulder's edge, keeping her eyes above sea level and focused.

Sing, her inner voice cried. Lure him in and sing, damn it!

Sucking in a deep breath, Serena pushed her face from the water and opened her mouth. She knew the haunting melody well; knew the lure her voice would have on the boy. Placing her hands on a jagged edge, she pushed around to see the male. His body stiffened, dropping the oars with a thunk. He grappled for the edge of the boat, his body betraying him as he cuffed a hand over the top of his left ear. His cerulean eyes scanned the water, scanned the fog that slowly crept from the Pass until he spotted her. A grin played on his handsome face as he released his hold of the boat and clasped his other ear. His body slackened as her enchantment failed. Serena furrowed her brows. She had most definitely not expected the boy to evade her haunting song.

"I haven't come all this way to listen to your bitch tunes, demon. I know who you are. I was told about the princess with the scarlet hair," the boy called out, his voice low and husky. "I've come to fetch you, princess."

"And what makes you think I am going to leave you without sacrifice, Prince Aaron," Serena asked, her voice carrying in the air. "I, too, know who you are. I've heard the stories about the prince that sails the seas with his merry band of pirates." Silence lingered between the pair.

"Your queen has made a deal with our king," Aaron replied.

"What's a deal when you're dead?" she countered.

"Kill me and the treaty between our species is void!" the boy growled back.

"You think we care about a treaty? Our numbers outrank yours. The sea is vast, we do not quake at your mere attempt to staunch bloodshed. Andover does not scare us."

"Then why did your queen beg us to stop? Why did she sell, you, her sister to me? Your numbers have dwindled, your ranks broken, and your queen inexperienced. Break our treaty? Ha! We'll break each and every last one of you," the boy snapped back.

Irritation flit through Serena at the boy's words and a snarl caught in her throat. He would break her? *Her?* In his dreams. First, she would rip his arms from his torso and then sever his ears from his head. She would then sing her "bitch tunes" and capsize his boats. And as the light faded from his stunning eyes, she would smile before tearing into his artery and watching him bleed out. His death would be torture. His death would be fun. He wanted to threaten her? Then damn his treaty. Damn both kingdoms. She'd make them all pay. She wanted to destroy Andover from afar, not within its very walls and certainly not as their queen.

Dipping beneath the water's glassy surface, Serena took one last glance at her home. She would return… *someday*. Serena gritted her teeth, bit back her anger and returned her attention to the boy.

She smiled, and she eyed the boat's dark shadow looming overhead and swam towards it. If her songs didn't work against this boy, then she would be a silent killer. The shadow came closer until Serena was beneath the small vessel, swimming slowly to the side. She slinked beside it, steadily rising out of the water. The boy's back was to her, and through his drenched shirt, she could see his muscles tensing. His body knew danger was near, but did he know how near?

"Call me a demon bitch again and I'll tear your limbs from your body and drink your delectable blood, human," Serena hissed before slinking back beneath the waves. She watched the prince turn, his hand fumbling for something at his side and she saw him wield a dagger. Serena could feel the magic roll from the blade. An enchantment the boy did not understand.

"Just get in my boat," he growled.

"And why would I do that?" she asked, popping up alongside him. The boat rocked as he shifted his weight, turning to face her.

"Because," was all he said.

"I'm not a servant you can boss around, nor am I your pet. You wanna tilly? Fine, we can tilly."

"Tilly?"

"It means fight, you dunderhead." The boy lowered his dagger and rubbed at his face with his free hand.

"I just told you I don't want to fight. I just told you I don't want to kill. All I want is to fetch you and fulfill my duty so that I can return home." Serena huffed a laugh.

"A princess takes orders from no one but the queen."

"And yet, your queen has signed a treaty between our kingdoms and you still challenge me." Serena paused, knowing she had been outwitted and sighed.

"I'll get in your damn boat," she sighed, "but if you try any funny business, I won't hesitate to kill you."

The boy sneered at her and waited. "Get in the boat." The boy rolled his eyes and sighed, something she would have done herself, and outstretched a hand towards the siren princess.

Serena stuck out her bottom lip and outstretched her hand, clasping it in the prince's. His muscles grew taut as he hoisted her above the water, into his vessel. Pulling her tail up to her chest, Serena stared back at the young man. He was handsome and serious, lean and yet young. She wondered what this boy did to be on the shit end of the stick voyaging out to get her.

"Did you draw the short straw, princeling? Or does the king always send his son to clean up his messes?"

"Piss off," he replied. "I don't owe you any explanation, sea scum. Just shut your fish face and keep quiet until we get back to the ship." Serena opened her mouth to retort, but quickly shut it and stared off into the water. She would kill him when he least expected it.

5

AARON

aron rolled his eyes as his muscles strained against the waves. Irritation rolled off of him at the siren's mere presence and she annoyed the piss out of him. He flicked his tongue over his canine as his mind wandered to a happier place. A place where he could shove his poisoned dagger into the girl's belly and watch her explode into sea foam. Disgust and bile lurched up his throat, stinging it. Aaron narrowed his eyes and sucked in a hefty breath of salty air and kept rowing. How could his father expect him to marry such a creature?

Inhale.

His father had doomed him and the entire kingdom.

Exhale.

He was going to be a failed king—one that went down in history as the worst thing to ever grace Andover. And for what? A fucking treaty? Aaron rowed harder, pushing his muscles into overdrive and sliced the boat through the waves. His muscles ached, begging him to stop, but he continued until he was in sight of the ship.

The *Camilla Delarose* had been a gift to Aaron on his

sixteenth birthday from a noble in court. The Duke of Alcovera had wished to marry his daughter, Camilla, to Aaron in exchange for his town's ships, giving King Marlow the remainder of the ships he needed for his armada. The king accepted the offer and gifted a ship to Aaron in his favor. Aaron smiled at the memory and how excited he'd been. Camilla had been excited too, having won the heart of the prince. His betrothal to the fair maiden was one he would gladly get behind. But then his father had double-crossed him two years later and accepted a peace treaty with Adrella and their greedy sea queen, interrupting and upending his entire life. Aaron sighed and gnashed his teeth together, grinding them until the pain he had become accustomed to, radiated through his jaw. *That was another lifetime ago.*

"He's back!" he heard the crew yell in the distance, snapping his attention back to the present.

"Looks like he has the fish broad with him!" another shouted. The siren crossed her arms across her chest and stuck out her bottom lip. She lifted her nose into the air. *If she wasn't a monster, she'd be pretty, maybe even prettier than Camilla,* Aaron thought. He smiled at the notion and watched as the siren turned towards him.

"Something funny, princeling?" she hissed.

"Nope," he replied quickly, watching the siren's lips pucker into a grimace. Silence carried through the air between them, a growing tension Aaron felt creeping up his spine. *Enchantress.* The siren opened her mouth as though she heard his thoughts but quickly closed it, leaving Aaron with the last word. Whatever retort she had on the tip of her tongue, she kept to herself.

Closing in on the ship, Aaron howled back, "Let down a rope and take the sea demon first. I want to make sure she doesn't escape or eat me when you aren't looking.

Besides, there's enough of you on deck to contain her," he called up to Konnor, one of the crew members.

"If I wanted to eat you, I would have done so already," the temptress snapped at him. Aaron stifled a laugh and rolled his eyes. He pushed to his feet, extending his arms out for balance as the boat swayed side to side, water splashing over the edge. When he secured his footing, Aaron turned his attention to the crew above. He watched as they carefully lowered down a rope. Aaron's fingers fumbled through the air, grasping for it. Catching a firm grip on it, he turned his attention back to the girl and stood. Outstretching his hands to his sides, he moved slowly in fear of capsizing the small vessel. The siren moved faster than lightning towards the young prince, lacing her fingers in a death grip on his collar, and she pulled. Aaron lurched forward, releasing a hiss as the rope bit into his skin. He was nose to nose with the siren. His heart hammered faster in his chest. He needed to react, pull out his dagger and plunge it deep within the beast's chest, but fear immobilized him. His eyes widened. He could see her teeth, small and razor-sharp like those of a shark as she smiled back at him. Her eyes blazed angrily into his and then nothing. Her stare became blank, indifferent and her grip on him slackened.

Confused, Aaron pushed away, his legs like jelly beneath him, and fell backward hard into the boat. Water sloshed over the side, cooling his sweat-slicked skin, soaking him to the core.

"Please," she whispered. "Don't tie that rope around me." Serena's mind whirled, racing back to her memory of Calix, to the nets that held him prisoner as the sailors above pulled him through the murky waters. She couldn't let him tie a rope around her. She couldn't be taken like Calix. Serena couldn't bear the memory. The look in

Calix's desperate eyes as she grabbed the trident from her sister and shoved it through his chest. *"Some secrets deserve to be kept within the family."*

"H-how," Aaron began but stopped. His fingers curled into fists as he cleared his throat, suppressing his fear the best way he could, and started over. "How else am I to get you aboard?" he asked.

"Can't you hold me while they hoist you up?" she asked. Aaron scrunched his face. He had no desire to hold a scaly fish beast in his arms.

"No," he stated, his voice dripping like ice.

"Please?" she whispered again, but before he could answer, the siren began to glow, emanating a light hazy blue as it enveloped her entire body. Then the worst scream Aaron had ever heard, roared from the beast.

6

SERENA

*S*omeone was screaming but they were so far away. She turned her head to look for the injured creature, but the only blue light that lit the nothingness surrounded her. She looked down at her palms, watching her scales flake and sizzle from her flesh, the smell catching in her wrinkling nose. Bile lurched up her throat, stinging her esophagus, gagging her. She looked down past her hands, at the tiny black threads laced in a shiny coating that laced up her bottom torso holding it together. She felt her lips part and heard her siren song wailing in the distance as the small threads pulled apart, one by one, splitting her tail into two parts. Dark purple blood sprayed from her body, splattering her body. Her eyes widened and the blue light around her faded away. Pain, there was so much pain and screaming and blood. Serena blinked, wishing away the horror and looked down.

Sodden wood bit at her skin, cool and pimpling it. Purple blood, darker than the delicious human-red blood, painted the floor. The hairs on her arms raised. Screams grew louder, her throat searing as she came to. Serena stopped and closed her lips. Her face soaked in salty tears. She choked back her sobs as her flesh transformed. Aramis had said the transformation would be painful, but she had never told her sister just how much.

When the light surrounding her dissipated, Serena was left with nothing but an exposed human form. The air, though warm, pricked at her skin. As if on cue, a slight breeze of salt and sea greeted her, lifting her ruby locks and kissing her flesh, pebbling it. Everything felt so dull in this form. She could no longer smell the sweetness the sea carried or understand the chatter of gulls as they squawked overhead. Her body felt heavy. Serena tried to stand, but her legs quaked beneath her weight. Her knees buckled and before she knew it, she was falling. She reached out, grasping at air when strong, tanned arms wrapped around her. Serena felt power ripple from them, as she stared into bright blue eyes.

Serena blinked.

Once.

Twice, at the prince holding her up and reached out to move a strand of dark hair from his eye. The prince's eyes widened as he stared at her and his body flinched. He moved, almost mechanically, and placed Serena on her feet.

"Easy, now," the prince cooed and removed his arm from around her. He looked her over with a wary glance and tilted his head towards the towering ship.

His eyes are kind, Serena thought. Though the rest of his face told another story. A story of hatred and disgust. For a brief moment, Serena wondered if she could ever survive this marriage. Could she be with someone who would hate her for the rest of her days? Her fingers curled into fists, digging her nails into her milky palms. Pain bit at her hand, but it was enough to push the invading thoughts from her mind. Serena sucked in a deep breath, feeling the air expanding in her lungs. She was so… mortal, now. And powerless. When she felt as though her lungs were going to explode, she released her breath and peered back to the prince through her hooded lashes.

"Why are you staring at me?" she asked, her voice coming out rougher than she had wanted. She watched the prince flinch and a flash of hurt cross his face. "Is there something you want to say?" she tried again.

Silence.

"You clearly want to say something, princeling. So out with it!" But the prince remained silent. Serena rolled her eyes, irritation growing with each passing second as she took a step towards Aaron. The prince's lips perked upward into a smirk as his cheeks took on a pink hue. His blue eyes shifted from Serena's face towards the water and then back to her face. Something thrummed inside the siren; her stomach knotted and flipped on itself and a warm feeling encompassed her. She hated it. Hated every-thing. Serena bit her lip and waited for an answer.

"Oy! Aaron, are ye going to send up the lass?" a voice called from above, tearing Serena's attention away from the fleeting moment. She looked up as her eyes took in the sight of an attractive male, slightly older than the prince, and waved. The male froze, squinting down at her. Aaron looked up at his shipmate and then back at Serena, averting his eyes from her body and spoke.

"I'm going to need you to hold on tight. Wrap your arms around my neck," he said. Serena felt his hand move around her waist and shifted.

"Move your hand any lower and I will break every bone in it," she warned. The prince stifled a laugh, his breath chilling on her skin as he leaned in closer to her.

"I wouldn't dream of it." Wrapping both arms around

the prince, Serena held on tight as he grabbed the rope with his other hand and gave it a violent tug. His body was hard against her own, covered in a thin layer of fabric. She could feel his muscles tense as he gripped the rope and held Serena tightly against him. Something hard poked at her leg and for a moment Serena smirked. If

The young prince hated her; his body was certainly betraying him.

Up and up they went and Serena watched as her home grew further away from her. Hands reached from above, grabbing the prince. The princeling's arms tightened around Serena as the crew tugged them over the edge, projecting them. Serena hit the ship deck hard and sharp, piercing pain wrought through her backside, exposing her form to the sailors.

"I thought ye said you were fetching a siren princess?" the beautiful male said to Aaron.

"I did… she is…" he stuttered and looked back to Serena, who noticed his eyes glisten as he took in her form. She observed the sweat on his brow and the tent in his trousers. The prince shifted uncomfortably, scratching his neck and averting his gaze down towards the deck.

"Looks like a naked whore if you ask me," the other male said quietly, his voice nothing more than a whisper carried on the breeze. Anger erupted through Serena at the male's words. Whore. Whore? Did he know who she was? Did he realize that despite being in human form, she could still rip him limb from limb? Gritting her teeth, Serena bit back the retort threatening her lips. She would teach the male a lesson at the right place and time, but now was hardly that. Aaron looked to his friend and smacked him on the arm before thrusting his shirt over his head. The prince's body shone in the midday's light, glimmering in a sheen layer of dew. Serena's heart hammered a little harder. He was beautiful. She gulped, watching as he approached her. Aaron took to one knee and thrust his shirt into Serena's bosom.

"Clothe yourself," he growled at her before standing. Serena watched him through slitted eyes, fisting her fingers through the holes in the worn fabric. It wasn't a nice shirt, but would be better than nothing, she supposed. Aaron's body twisted under muscle. He turned, eyeing her up before smirking. Serena flashed the prince a toothy grin before cupping her exposed breasts and releasing an enjoyable moan. She watched as the Prince's body betrayed him again and his gaze flickered away from her. The crew snickered and whistled at the siren, calling for her to do far worse things. The prince glanced at her a final time before saying, "Do you enjoy the attention, Princess? Because like everything in this world, it will be taken away."

Serena grumbled as she leaned against the side of the ship. The wood wet and cool against her hot flesh. She had never been ill before, especially not from the waves, but as the ship lifted and sank with each wave that caressed the vessel, Serena grew sicker. Her stomach knotted and stabbed pain through her like the fury of a thousand sirens as she hurled up bile.

"Well would ya look at that," a familiar voice sounded from Serena's side. She shut her eyes, relishing the wind whipping her face and wiped her mouth with the back of her hand. "Aren't you supposed to be immune to seasickness?" Prince Aaron asked, leaning down on his forearms and staring out into the vast nothingness. The stench gagged Serena as she ralphed again, spewing bile into the sea below.

"Don't you have better things to do rather than hassling me?" Serena grumbled. Aaron huffed a laugh and then sighed.

"I was sent to fetch you. You are my only priority."

"Well, it may prove that your priorities leave you in an unfortunate position," Serena sneered.

"Why's that?"

"Because I am going to kill you and your crew." Moving with the speed of the sea, Serena reached over and grabbed the prince by the throat. Her nails pierced his tanned skin, dripping scarlet drops down onto his chest.

"Release me," Aaron wheezed. "Or you will die. Right here, Right now."

"I hardly think you're in a position to be demanding anything from me right now," Serena hissed.

Something sharp poked into Serena's spine. She spun the prince in tow and was greeted by the cool glint of metal to her throat.

"Hello, Serena," a female voice greeted, freezing the siren in her tracks.

7

SERENA

"Mystic Brooksborough," Serena hissed through clenched teeth. The raven-haired woman smirked at the princess. Serena was no fool. She knew when she'd been beat(en) and knew if she didn't back away now, she would die. Unfurling her fingers, she released her grip on the prince's throat. She'd heard many stories in the crystal kingdom about Mystic, "Blade of the Adrellan Seas", "Siren Slayer." Her blood boiled looking into the dark irises of her foe. Her skin was dark like the midnight sky and bore scars from Serena's fallen kin. Her hair was tied in knotted braids atop her head, spilling down her back. She wore nothing special, knee-high black boots, a white linen tunic, and dark pants. But what caught Serena's eye was all of the slayer's weapons–daggers holstered at her hip, a stiletto strapped to the inner side of her boot, and her blade's sheath strapped to her back. The slayer bore a scowl, darting her eyes over towards Aaron. Serena gulped, watching as the blade's tip nearly grazed her neck and followed the pirate's gaze. The prince rubbed at his neck, still red from her grip.

"Do- do you two know each other?" he asked. His eyes widened, darting between the two women as he mindlessly continued to rub his neck.

"Where are your daggers?" the slayer huffed towards the prince. "I gave them to you in case I was indisposed, which I clearly was."

"They're away."

"Away where?" the pirate pressed on.

Serena refused to blink.

Refused to take her eyes off of the pirate.

"Siren Slayer," she snarled, baring her serrated teeth.

"Not now, monster."

She wished she could spit venom at the pirate, wished that trait hadn't died out throughout the ages. But only the Mer could spit venom, and those were creatures that had long been banished from the Adrellan Seas. Dark and dangerous, the Mer sought to destroy both man and siren alike and take the sea and the Pass for themselves, killing anything and anyone that crossed their paths. But Serena's grandfather had banished them, giving them the seas past the Pass and all of the lands(,thereof). Giving them a place to call home. It had been a while since Serena had thought of the Mer, and at this moment she wished she could call upon her cousins and slay the slayer.

"Remove your blade from the siren's neck," Aaron said. Serena could see the disdain etched on the slayer's face. How she probably wished to sink the blade deep within Serena.

"Ay," Mystic answered. "The seas are safer with me aboard a ship and my siren's blade at my hip," she replied, sheathing her sword. Serena's fingers clenched into fists, aching as her nails plunged into her palms. Purple blood pooled to the surface, staining her nails and dripping into the wooden floorboards below. But she paid no mind to it, barely wincing at the pain.

"You killed many of my kin. I should tear your arms from their sockets and choke the life from your lungs. And now you stand with a blade to my neck and threaten to kill me for touching my betrothed."

"You are not the only one here against their will, Princess. My liege," Mystic nodded towards the prince, "has spared my life to ensure his life and the Treaty carries on. So, should you threaten his life, or dare I even say, your own, I will be here to intervene. Threaten any of the crew, and my blade will taste siren blood once more. Better get used to me, Princess. I am here for the long haul." Serena dug her nails in deeper as hatred seeped through her soul. Another name to add to her death note. Another wrong she would right and another body to fill her aching belly. The slayer turned, her boots echoing as they thunked along the deck boards away from Serena and Aaron. Serena looked over at the prince and glared.

"Please," she began. "Show me to my chamber so that I may sleep this nightmare away." His eyebrows flashed upwards and without a word, Aaron grabbed for her uninjured hand before tugging her behind him.

Serena's cabin was nothing fancy, just four bare wooden walls and a cot to call her own, which was more than most of the crew had. A small candle hung from the wall, casting shadows. Serena was finally alone. Pulling the linen shirt over her head, Serena discarded it onto the ground and blew out the candle. It took a moment for her eyes to adjust before she climbed into her cot with nothing to cover her but a thin flat piece of fabric the humans called a sheet.

How strange, she thought, lying on her back staring up at the ceiling. She felt the ship rise and fall with the waves, lulling her into oblivion. Did every human do this? Lie aimlessly, helplessly in the dark waiting for their body to just give up? She wanted the nightmare to end, wanted to wake up back in her chambers at the crystal castle, and as her muscles ached and her body stiffened on her cot, her lashes fluttered. Sleep greeted the siren princess like an old friend as she drifted into a dreamless slumber.

8

AARON

$\mathcal{A}$aron watched the sun dip towards the horizon as it painted the sky in rich streaks of reds, oranges, and deep purples. The eve was upon them and his home was growing near. The ship sailed at full capacity, every deckhand working, thrusting the ship through easy waters. Andover was growing closer, the lands for which he was named. Specks of gold glinted in the distance, a shimmer of the castle his father had built long ago, flooding his vision. Aaron clenched his teeth. Upon his return would be his engagement announcement to the siren scum. Gods, he could just picture Camilla's sweet face seething at the news. He loved her. Gods, did he love her. She was the sweetest girl in court. Aaron's eyes softened as he imagined her smile, large and innocent, but he knew better than that. She was far from innocent and it was his undoing.

Flowers decorated the arches of the halls as Aaron stood with Petar, not hearing a word that escaped the pirate's lips, distracted by the beauty that stood mere feet away from him. Her dark luscious locks glittered in the low light of the sconces, curling down her back in a sea of waves. She wore a dress of lavender, the perfect shade to complement her porcelain shoulders.

Aaron felt his heart thudding uncontrollably in his chest. Surely, it would break a rib or two, attempting to escape. His mouth went dry, his tongue like sandpaper as the girl turned. Camilla Delarose, marquess of Alcovera, daughter of the Duke, heir to an armada, military and sacred trade routes stared at him from under long lashes. Her lips quirked and her large doe-like eyes widened as her cheeks took on a pink hue. She turned her head towards the other courtesans, whispering something Aaron couldn't hear and then moved towards him. Aaron tried to swallow, but the lump in his throat choked him. His mouth was like a godsdamned desert. Camilla closed in, her fingers fumbling with her skirts as she curtsied.

"How do you do, Your Majesty?" she asked, looking up at him through hooded lashes.

"I'm better now that you're here, my lady," he crooned, taking her hand to his lips.

HE HAD TO BREAK IT TO HER BEFORE SHE HEARD AT THE ball. He owed her that much at least. He'd left without so much as a goodbye to her. Without so much as a kiss. But his father had made it clear that he was to leave immediately and fetch the fish. And there was no talking back to the king, not unless he wanted to hurt more than he already did.

Perhaps he could work out a deal to have her as the siren's lady? Then he wouldn't have to stop seeing her. They could still be together in the ways of man and woman, just... secretly. Taking a deep breath, Aaron let out a sigh unaware of the company sidled up next to him.

"What troubles yer mind?" Petar asked quietly, staring

out into the distance. Aaron turned, resting his arm along the ship's side; his attention held by the captain.

"Women," Aaron replied.

"Aye, lasses have always been the conflict of a man's heart."

"Indeed, they have. But I think my conflict is a bit more than what my heart wants."

"Yer conflict is about the siren broad, ay?" Petar asked, fishing into his dark coat pocket and procuring a smoke. He lifted the tobacco to his lips and lit the end. Smoke billowed into the air, choking Aaron as his friend took another drag and passed the smoke to him.

"It will help," Petar reassured him as Aaron lifted the tobacco to his lips. He sucked in, allowing the smoke to fill his lungs and a rush to coat his thoughts. He exhaled as the smoke began to burn his lungs. His racing thoughts slowed as did a bit of his world.

"What's in your smoke, Cap'n?" Aaron asked, growing a bit dizzy.

"Only the good stuff," he replied. Aaron stared back out into the smooth waters below. He felt the wind lick at his face and closed his eyes for a moment.

Lips brushed against his in the moonlight, the cool breeze of autumn biting at their skin, but Aaron didn't care. He was with the fairest girl of them all. Camilla. His heart skipped a beat as his lips stole kisses in the night. If they were caught, it wouldn't be good. But they had yet to be seen. Countless kisses and stolen moments had led to this moment.

"Marry me," he breathed against Camilla's lips. "Let me give you the world." Camilla stilled, her large eyes looking up to him.

"Okay," she whispered.

"Okay?"

"Yes, Aaron. I'll marry you, though we were predestined to be with one another. Ships for me. Don't you remember?"

"I remember. But your love is worth more than any armada. I don't want a loveless marriage."

"I love Camilla, ya know. This whole thing just isn't fair," he said, opening his lids. As if his words moved something within the captain, Petar moved and pulled the prince into a deep hug. Aaron could feel his friend's breath on his ear as he whispered, "Sometimes ya have to take one fer the team. What's good fer the kingdom may not always be what's best for ye. Make do. Make do." Petar held him tightly against his chest before pulling away and smiled.

"Now, I have the siren slayer aboard the ship. It's not often we have women accompany us. If ye excuse me, Highness, I need to see what else she can slay, if ya know what I mean." Aaron chuckled a bit and slapped his friend on the shoulder.

"Good luck, Cap'n," he replied, flashing his friend a devilish smile. Petar winked and retreated towards the cabins.

9

MYSTIC

*M*ystic sat at the dingy bar held a few floors below deck, taking in the rancid smell of stale ale and unbathed men. The room was dimly lit from enclosed sconces hanging on the wall, their flames shielded from the wood. Shadows danced around the room, casting a mysterious glow to the surrounding patrons. Mystic lifted her crystal mug to her dry, chapped lips and closed her eyes, relishing the sour taste of her drink. She listened to the kitchen crew tell stories of their previous adventures when the door behind her pushed open. Mystic lowered her mug, the glass landing with a *clink* against the bar and turned.

The crew's laughter died as a dark figure emerged through the beaten, ale-stained door. The captain, reeking of smoke, stumbled inside in a haze, smiling like an oaf. Tripping over his booted feet, he pulled up a stool to the bar next to Mystic. She *nearly* choked from his odor as she took another swig. The slayer wasn't sure if the captain had helped himself to ale beforehand or if his smoke was laced with something far more powerful than it gave off. He plunked in the seat and ordered up a shot for himself. She felt her nose wrinkle in disgust and tried to pull some form of politeness from within her. She was, after all, a guest on his ship. She had to remain in his good graces if she were to steal the delectable captain's boat. He would never know what happened until it was too late.

"Do you like riding my vessel?" The captain slurred, swigging back a shot of whiskey. He puckered his lips and slammed his glass down with force, sliding it back across the bar to the barkeep for another. "Keep 'em coming, and a round for the bonnie lass as well," he said, giving Mystic a wink. The slayer rolled her dark eyes. She wasn't unaccustomed to men trying and failing to charm her. It happened in every port town she was in and a ship full of men rendered no different. She was aware of the stares men gave her and how pretty she appeared to them. Her mother had once joked she could have been part siren for the enchantment she put on males, but Mystic had always thought that as an insult.

Damn them all to the deepest depths, if that's what they thought she was.

She blinked back her intruding thoughts and flashed a smile at the captain. He was handsome, she could give him that much. He had flaxen hair, bright blue eyes and pale skin, slightly reddened by the sun. He was dressed in a white billowy linen shirt that refused to give anything of his form away to her, and tawny pants, the same shade as her skin. It had sure been a while since she'd lain with any man and Mystic was sure if she wanted to bag the captain, she certainly could. Batting her thick lashes, Mystic decided to work her magic and talk this man into bed with her.

"Aye," she replied in confirmation. "You have a nice boat here. Now, do you lay it on thick with every woman aboard the ship or just me?" The captain's milky complexion took on a pink hue in the cheeks, either from embarrassment or flattery, Mystic didn't know. He sidled in closer to her; the creak of his chair groaning against the dark wooden floorboards.

"Only ye," he nearly whispered in a voice so low and full of husk. He leaned in closer to the slayer until she could feel his whiskey breath on her cheek. Her body groaned with lust as she focused on his mouth and the curve of his lips. She wondered what they would feel like against hers.

"Why?" she demanded, a little harsher than she had intended it to be. Two glasses clinked on the bar, momentarily tearing Mystic's attention away from the captain to the amber liquid flowing into them. A strong urge to drink both beckoned to her. To her demons. The barkeep slid the glass with fluid easily across the bar and Mystic stopped it, like old times. She lifted the glass to her nose and breathed in the rich flavors of alcohol before casting a side glance to her ship companion. The captain smiled at her and raised his glass in a toast. Her stomach fluttered in response like small butterflies trying to escape.

"To Andover and pretty women," he said, downing the glass and sliding it back over to the keep. He winked one beautiful eye at the slayer and she smiled. *Gods, he was charming and stunning to look at.* As the alcohol settled into her belly, the fuzzy warm feeling of her demons awakening cast over her.

"To Andover and drunk men," she cooed back before tipping her glass and head back, reeling in the glorious burn of the whiskey as it trailed down her throat. She slid her glass back over to the keep. "If I didn't know it, Captain, I'd say you were trying to get me drunk to have your way with me." The captain's lips spread into a wide flirtatious grin before he finished his third shot of whiskey.

"Who says I'm not?"

Mystic laughed as her body grew warmer and her head fuzzier. The barkeep sent another shot her way. Raising her glass in the air, she winked at the captain and said, "Well then, to drunken rolls in the sack." She downed her shot.

MYSTIC AWOKE STRIPPED TO HER BARE FORM AS THE SOUND of snoring erupted from beside her. Her head ached with pounding pains as she glanced over at the captain and smiled. He had been a fun distraction, something she had needed. She rose to dress, her body aching in all the right places as she pulled her own linen shirt over her head. Mystic fastened her siren's blade to her back before thrusting her boots over her bare feet. Her footsteps echoed across the floorboards as she exited the captain's messy chamber. The cabin hall was empty as Mystic wandered back to the deck, the lights of a few lit sconces shadowing the way. She hadn't cared about her appearance really. It was likely the crew knew their leader had bedded her.

Daylight beckoned the horizon, casting an orangey glow down the deck steps. Mystic squinted, the light hurting her eyes as she looked around the deck and out into the ocean. The *Camilla Rose* sliced through the waves as though they were a hot knife through butter and landed them closer to Andover. Mystic's lips perked as she spotted the hazy outline of the city and the sharp glint of the golden castle. The last time she had been there, she had caused havoc in the pubs and throughout Lower town, where all of Andover's finest scuttled. She remembered the look on the Chief of Police's face as she hustled him out of a week's pay. He had warned her never to show her face in Lower town again. Little did he know that this time she would be pardoned by none other than the king himself. All of her mishaps had been pardoned, and that brought pure joy to the pirate's heart. She would swindle and sleep with the richest of men and then would hustle them too.

"Land Ho!" the captain's second bellowed from the deck above. Movement clattered from the cabins beneath them and footsteps clattered up the wooden steps onto the deck. The captain emerged last, grinning as he spotted Mystic and gave her a knowing wink. She felt the blood rush into her cheeks and heat them but could do nothing to stop it. He'd been a winner, one of the best she'd been with and would likely remain so for a long while. Pirate men, captains nonetheless, certainly knew their way around a woman's body. She watched as the captain began to command his crew and offered up her services.

"Aye," Petar responded, "but ye will need to don some trousers if ye wish to help the crew. Can't have them distracted now." Mystic felt blood rush into her cheeks again as embarrassment washed over her and looked down. She was indeed pantless.

"Shit," she cursed. "I'll be back." She disappeared down the steps towards the captain's private quarters.

SERENA

*S*erena dreamed of the sea, of the waves and the fish, but mostly of her home and the friends she'd left behind. There was noise, a loud noise that gripped and shook her world. Serena's eyes shot open, spotting a dark figure before her. Her insides rumbled and ached, knotting in on themselves as the stranger came into focus. A short round man stood before her. No one she recognized as she took in his round face and stubble. His dark eyes were rimmed with bags and circles as though he hadn't slept in days, and his body was in need of a bath. Her nose wrinkled at his ungodly stench.

"Cap'n said the prince is needin' to see ya, miss," he drawled. "Land ho, miss." Serena blinked, hardly registering the rotund figure's words and stretched her arms up towards the ceiling. Her dreams were better than this godforsaken hell she had been sold into. Bones cracked and popped as the princess rose, towering over the dingy crewmate. His eyes widened as they raked down her body, drinking in her naked form. Serena smiled. Taking a step forward, she watched as he grew excited and took a step back towards the door. Serena crooked her head to the side and smirked. She would have fun with the bloke. Biting her bottom lip, her tooth broke open the wound that formed during her meeting with the siren slayer, pouring blood into her mouth once more. She extended her tongue, lapping it up as her stomach grumbled. She would need to eat… soon. And no one would miss the sorry excuse of a man standing before her becoming excited.

"What is your name?" she asked, her predatory side closing in on its prey. The sailor stumbled backward some more, jumping at her words. His back crashed against the wooden door and the smallest squeak burst from his lips.

"W-what?"

"Your name?" she asked again, taking a coy step towards him.

"Konnor, miss." The name played like music in her ears, singing to her soul. Konnor. The name of her last human meal.

"Do you like music, Konnor?" she asked, taking another step forward. The sailor merely nodded and gulped; his body tensed as Serena lifted her nose into the air. Adrenaline coursed through the man's veins, seeping from his pores like honey. Serena's smirk grew wider as she poised herself to sing.

"Come with me and then you'll see," Serena began to sing, twirling towards her victim, reaching her hands up towards the decks above. *"For a child of the sea I was born to be."* She twirled, closing the gap between her and Konnor, kneeling to his level. She pushed her breasts into him, feeling him, tasting his breath before grazing her lips along his. *"Die you must, to join us. In my haunting melody."* Serena pushed her lips against Konnor's tasting his fear, his beautiful, wonderful fear, and his enchantment. She pulled away.

He was hers.

Within her grasp.

She looked into his eyes, eyes filled with wonder and lust and awe.

"Konnor?" she asked in a tone far from innocent. "Would you like to die?"

She knew what the answer would be.

The song had enchanted him.

"For you, I'd do anything," he breathed.

"Such a good boy," Serena whispered, her lips trailing from his down to his neck where his carotid artery pumped with his life force. She felt a shudder course through Konnor, and then she sank her serrated teeth into his neck. Blood wept into her mouth as she sank them deeper into Konnor's flesh. He let out a yelp, but Serena allowed him to feel his death and she relished in it. There would be no need to stifle his screams, he would be dead in a moment's time. She pulled back, watching the light fade from Konnor's eyes before diving in to finish the sailor off.

Serena emerged from her cabin, licking the last bits of Konnor from her fingers as she ascended the cabin hall's steps. She was dressed in a warm white linen tunic and a pair of brown trousers that tapered off just past her knees. Her exposed skin pebbled from the cool morning breeze, but Serena didn't mind. With her belly full, thanks to Konnor, she felt as though her new adventure may be the beginning of a beautiful massacre. Konnor had been delectable and it would be ages, if ever, when they would find his remains. She had finished him until nothing was left of the sailor, but a few bones. He sat like a rock in her belly and it would be a long time before she would need to eat again. Though her next meal would be human food. A smile played on her lips as she imagined Andover's streets running red, crumpled bodies draining into the streets and all the humans she could eat. Her smile continued to grow into a devious grin as she watched the crew flounce around on deck.

"Where's Konnor? We're home." The prince's voice sounded from beside her, tearing Serena from her glorious daydream. She jumped, caught off guard by his presence and narrowed her eyes.

"You're home. I will never see mine again," Serena replied, avoiding the question, and watched as Andover came into view and a part of her heart broke. She would be land bound. Cool fingers laced between hers, giving her hand a gentle squeeze. Serena froze and looked up, yanking her hand back. The prince's eyes saddened as his face dropped

"I know it's not your home," he nearly whispered. "But I hope someday you will love Andover as much as I do. I pray you will give it a chance. Give me a chance and I will try to give you the world."

"Praying is for fools," Serena hissed, whirling to face the prince. "You want to make me happy?"

"Yes," the prince replied. "More than anything, I want this treaty to work."

"Then take me back to my godsdamned home." Pain flared in the prince's face, replaced by something hard and unreadable. Serena watched his jaw clench before he spoke.

"If you want to be miserable, then there is nothing I can give you. Nothing I can do for you. If you want to be miserable, then you can rot alone in a cold cell until death takes you." The finality of his words struck Serena like a blow to the gut. There would be no bargaining. No lavish life or glimpses of the sea. She knew if she wanted a chance to go home, then she would need to make nice. Play the prince to slay the king. And she would play. Letting out a sigh, Serena bowed her head.

"Fine," she said. "Show me the world and all the mumbo jumbo you blather on about." The Prince flashed his pearly whites, though his eyes still mirrored a sadness. A pang gnawed in Serena's gut. Was it pity? Pity for herself or for the prince? She didn't know. Serena extended her hand, and the prince accepted, enveloping her fingers within his own.

"Welcome to Andover, Princess Serena of Adrella."

THOUSANDS OF PEOPLE FLANKED THE DOCKS AS THE *Camilla Delarose* pulled into port; hollers and cries of joy welcomed the prince and Serena as the ship anchored. The crew bustled around deck, each shouting over the next; the roar deafening in the siren's ears. Serena's eyes widened, taking in the view. Buildings of all shapes, sizes, and colors sat nearly atop of one another. She had never seen a city so bright. Banners of gold and red hung from the windows and children played throughout the cobbled streets, or at least the ones Serena could see. The women wore lavish, rich-colored gowns, most adorned with some variation of white, gold or red and flowers in their hair.

The men wore suits in shades of purple and blue that Serena had only seen paint the sky as the sun set below the horizon. The air smelled of the ocean breeze, salty sea, and fish essence. Waves crashed against the rocks as they came to shore.

The prince squeezed her hand once more, his rough fingers grazing overtop of her soft hand. Serena bristled silently to herself and forced a smile to her lips.

"Relax," the prince murmured. "These people will welcome you with open arms as they do me." Serena rolled her eyes.

"Because you're the heir to the throne," she said. Her heart hammered in her chest and Serena felt her chest tighten. She wanted to breathe, but only small puffs of air entered her lungs. The prince squeezed her fingers in response before turning to her. His eyes were unreadable as he moved in close to her. His nose was mere inches from her own and if she wanted, she could have torn his throat out in seconds with only her bare teeth, right in front of his own people. That would knock him down a peg and put him in his rightful place.

"Act like a princess. Wave to the people. Be kind, or I swear I will lock you up with Brooksborough and let her have ten minutes alone with you, sea scum. I am trying my best to play the role of loving Prince Aaron, happy fiancé to the siren bitch. Know. Your. Role," Aaron spat, spittle flecking Serena's face and lip; her eyes closing reflexively. Serena took a step back; her head spinning as she imagined the death blow she would serve the prince. An uppercut to the jaw and a twist of his neck. She wiped his spit from her face with the sleeve of her tunic and squeezed the prince's hand hard. Casting a glance down, Serena watched their fingers grow from red to white, her own fingers aching in response as she forced another smile to her face.

"Oh, I know my role," she hissed.

"Good," was all the prince said before he surged forward without warning, yanking Serena behind him down the walkway to the docks. Her feet stumbled beneath her, tripping over wooden flanks. Hands reached for the siren princess as she stepped onto land. Her eyes furrowed, feeling the sand beneath her feet. Warm and yet soft. Was everything the land held, warm? She stopped and released Aaron's hand, watching him as he flew forward, tumbling to his knee. He righted himself and dusted off his pants before turning to face her. His bright eyes narrowed and the muscles in his arms flexed as he crossed them.

"So sorry, my liege," she purred. Her lips perked upwards, and she knew malice played on her lips. Know her role? Ha! She knew how to play the whole damn kingdom.

The crowd grew in size, circling the crew, Aaron, and Serena as more people flooded in. They watched the princess intently, muttering words of confusion and disdain. But Serena didn't care. A laugh stifled from her throat as she squished her toes between the sand.

"What in the gods' names are you doing?" Aaron growled.

"Becoming one with the land," Serena replied. "You should try it sometime. You might find that you like it." The prince's body tensed and his eyes shot daggers at the siren. But Serena did not care. If he wanted to be a grump, then that was on him.

Serena watched Aaron furl and unfurl his fingers towards his palms and moved her gaze to his face—his cold, stony face. Angered flared through his eyes. *Gotcha.*

"Is something funny to you, Princess?" The prince bristled. "Please by all means share with us your thoughts. I'm sure the people would like to know." Aaron's voice rose to a shout as he walked in a large circle towards the crowd. The murmurs around them grew and people began to push and shove their way closer.

Serena flicked her tongue over her serrated canine and grinned wildly.

Game on.

She took a step towards the prince as he rounded her

way and lowered her voice so that only he could hear
here.

"I'm playing my role," she hissed before turning to face
the crowd. She would enchant them, win over their hearts
and their minds. Serena stepped away from the prince and
parted her lips. And then she began to sing.

MYSTIC

The siren's lips parted as Mystic stepped foot onto Andoverian soil. A melody so sweet erupted from the princess and Mystic felt her own body relax. One by one, the crowd succumbed to the Siren's enchantment; bodies around her began to slacken. Mystic moved, quicker than she had ever done, fighting against the temptress's tune, and clasped her hands over the top of her ears. The muffled sound eased Mystic's body and her eyes began to droop. She closed her eyes and focused on her breathing. Her father had taught her this. She knew what to do, how to fight.

"Remember to breathe, slow and steady. And then when you're centered, strike. If you wait any longer, you'll be a puppet to the tune. You're better off dead at that point." Her father's words played through her mind. Mystic knew she would have to act fast and silence the siren without death if that were even possible. She willed herself to breathe, easy steady breaths before opening her eyes.

These people were now at the siren's beck and call. If the enchantress wanted them to die, all she had to do was sing it and it would be done. Mindless zombies enchanted by ancient spells that came from the monster's lips. Silently, Mystic padded, placing her weight to the sides of her feet as she crept alongside the docks, weaving in and out of the frozen crewmates. She halted, mere steps from the docks as she spotted Petar. His feet were planted in place as he swayed to the music. She moved quickly to his side and grabbed ahold of his swaying form with one hand, exposing her ear to the siren's voice.

"Snap out of it," she hissed into Petar's ear, before slapping her hand back over her own. His eyes flicked towards her, but his body continued to sway.

It was no use.

He was too far gone.

A puppet stuck in its husk.

Mystic wanted to yell. She wanted to scream and hit and throw things at everyone. She wanted to snap them from their demonic trances, but it would be of no use. As long as the siren bitch breathed, she would enchant the kingdom.

Win their minds.

Mystic narrowed her gaze, watching the siren twirl in and out of the crowd. Her arms reached towards the sun, moving in fluid grace with her song. Mystic knew she needed to get to the siren and stop her from enchanting the entire kingdom. She couldn't slay her. At least not without breaking the treaty and placing a death order upon herself. But she would be damned if she let the siren brainwash and eat these people or worse.

No. Don't go there, she told herself. She wondered if that was the princess's plan all along. To kill the kingdom in order to free herself. Mystic shook her head. *No, too easy.*

Every man, woman, and child stood frozen in place as Mystic crept closer. The slayer gulped down the hard lump forming in her throat and continued towards the siren in her crouched stance. Tears pricked at her eyes and her knees ached, begging for relief. But there was no rest for the wicked and she would be relieved when she silenced the beast. Her heart hammered against her ribcage, threatening to break free and she felt like she needed to pee.

Mystic quickened her pace and headed straight for the siren. Serena's back was turned to her as she continued to move; her hips gliding them back and forth in rhythm as she picked at her tunic, exposing her midriff to the crowd. Teasing them. Tempting them.

Temptress.

Slowly, Mystic removed one hand from her ear, fighting against the song that threatened to take hold of her and drew her siren's blade from her back. She crept towards the princess, tightening her hand on her hilt until she was mere feet from the siren.

"Stop!" Mystic called out. "Or I'll gut you right here, right now." The siren froze, silencing as she turned to face the slayer. Mystic felt her lips curl, felt the smile snake onto her face as she watched a plethora of emotions cross Serena's.

"Drop your weapon, Brooksborough," the siren snarled. Mystic's fingers curled tighter until her knuckles turned white and her palms hurt. She swallowed.

"Not going to happen."

"Must we do this?" Serena asked, dropping her hands from their skyward position.

"We must."

"Well, get on with it. What do you want? Can't you see I'm performing for my kingdom?"

"Do you plan on honoring the treaty or should I kill you right here and now?" Mystic growled. Anger flared in the siren's eyes as she flashed her pearly whites at the pirate. Her serrated fangs glinting in the sunlight. Mystic had the beast right where she wanted her.

"You better watch yourself, slayer," she said, narrowing her eyes. "I'm here on my own volition, to join our two kingdoms. I don't intend to break that promise. But stab me through the heart and watch how fast the dark tides turn."

"Cute play on words, demon." But Mystic knew it wasn't a play on words, but the truth. She gulped, her heart thrumming hard in her chest as a chill ran through the slayer. She had two options. One, kill the beast and break the treaty, but then she'd be on the king's hit list, or two, let the temptress live and keep a close eye out.

Mystic lowered her blade, choosing the latter as murmurs echoed through the crowd, each person snapping from the siren's enchantment.

"That is enough!" Aaron's voice hissed from behind them. Mystic turned on her booted heel and peered into the prince's angry face. She wasn't sure when he moved, but he took a step between her and the beast. His fists clenched at his sides and set his jaw.

"You are done here, Brooksborough."

"But—" she began.

"If you threaten Serena again," he cut in, "then you threaten all of Andover."

"You can't be serious."

"I stand behind the princess and my words. Threaten her again and your head will be mine."

Mystic felt the blood drain from her face. She felt the tremble in her hands as anger raged through her body. Her head swam and vision blurred. She clenched her jaw and cocked her face to the side, narrowing her eyes.

"You're going to regret this," she sneered, watching as Aaron's brows rose.

"Is that a threat?" he asked coolly.

"No, it's a promise." She licked at her teeth and gazed back into the prince's eyes as she sheathed her blade.

"Get out of my sight before I take your tongue."

"Fine," was all she said before turning on her heel, pushing into the crowd.

SERENA

Blood rushed through Serena's ears, drowning her in a sea of doubt and despair. Being in a new kingdom was terrifying and *exciting*. People wanted to meet *her*, but not everyone in the kingdom was welcoming. Some smiled and clasped hands with the princess, while others shot her nasty glances and shouted ill words. She'd been escorted in a covered carriage drawn by two large four-legged beasts whose dark hair ran down their choco-late necks. The sounds of their feet clopped on the cobbled street below, shaking the caravan.

Prince Aaron sat in a red velveted seat across from Serena, staring blissfully out the window. Sunlight poured through the caravan windows, shadowing the prince's features from the siren. But every now and then, he would raise his hand and wave to the citizens of Andover. She watched the natives beam and coo praises to Aaron before returning to their duties.

Serena had so much to learn and so many questions. She bit her lower lip, contemplating what to ask as the silence between her and the prince lingered.

"The noise," Serena began, curling her fingers as she cleared her throat, "what is it?"

"What noise?"

"The clippety-clop." The prince huffed out a sigh and rubbed at his face, muttering something under his breath that Serena couldn't make out. She narrowed her eyes.

"Well?" she asked, growing annoyed with each passing second.

"Hooves," Aaron replied.

"Hooves?" she pressed, her voice trailing up an octave. "What is a hoof?" She watched as the prince visibly clenched his fists and let out a groan.

"They belong to the horses pulling the carriage, Princess," he said, exasperated before returning his gaze out the window. Serena sucked in a breath, keeping her gaze on the prince the entire way to the castle. He couldn't wish her gone. After all, he'd been the one to bring her here. But she would be damned if she let him ignore her. She would get her answers, learn his ways, and then when he least expected it, she would kill him.

It wasn't long before the carriage slowed, bringing the golden castle into sight. Serena's words caught in her throat as she took in the sheer size of her new home.

"Once we're out, go away. I'll send for you when I'm ready."

"Excuse you? I'm not a peasant you can call upon and send away as you please. I'm…" She rested her hand upon her chest.

"Shut it," Aaron hissed. "I'll send for you. I have things to tend to."

"Things?"

"Gods! You're so annoying! Just go roam the castle. I'll find you!"

"Whatever," Serena mumbled as the wagon stopped

abruptly. The door beside them lurched open. Serena couldn't see who had opened it, just that it was open to a new and vast world. Aaron stood, slowly descending the steps before holding out a hand for the princess. She rose and bit back her pride as she wrapped her hand within his and was helped down.

"Remember, I'll come find you," he said before disappearing into a throng of people, leaving Serena completely and utterly alone.

AARON

This wasn't going to be easy. Although, breaking hearts rarely was. Aaron had left Serena alone. A gutsy move, he knew, especially when that fish was a stone-cold killer. But what other choice did he have? He couldn't exactly waltz around with Serena on his arm while telling Cam everything. The thought was preposterous.

His footfalls echoed through the corridors leading to the guest rooms. He knew Cam would be there, likely getting ready for the party. Everyone was likely getting ready. The halls were empty, no souls in sight, not even chambermaids. Aaron sucked in a breath as he clambered towards Camilla's door. His lungs burned as his fingers grazed the cool metal handle before dropping his hand back to his side.

Aaron let out a sigh and dropped his chin to his chest. Yes, he loved her. But he loved his kingdom more. Perhaps heartbreak was the only way to spare what feelings they both had. Perhaps, having her loathe him would be better than the broken look on her face. He couldn't do this. Turning on his heel, Aaron retreated from whence he came. He had a fish to find and a duty to behold. The only heart breaking, was his.

SERENA

Ironclad sconces hung from the slate painted walls every ten feet, illuminating the corridors in an orangey glow. Serena prowled, noting how odd it was that the halls were empty as she waited for Aaron to retrieve her. She neared the end of one corridor and started down another when her breath hitched. Paintings lined the corridor to her left and right, faces of royals long since passed; each dressed to the nines and immortalized. Names etched on golden placards hung under the paintings, but Serena was not fluent in Andoverian and couldn't read them, though she desperately wished she could. This was her home now. Her fingers traced the cool nameplate hanging below a woman with white-blonde hair and shockingly familiar blue irises.

Slowly, she reached out, grazing her fingers along the painting. Serena closed her eyes and imagined the woman before her. *Was she kind or malevolent? Strict or easy-going?* Consumed in her own thoughts, Serena's mind whirled.

"She's beautiful, isn't she?" a familiar voice asked, echoing around her. Serena tensed, her muscles growing taut as she opened her lids. She gnashed her teeth together and flexed her jaw.

Prince Aaron.

His footsteps reverberated through the corridor as he approached. Serena flicked her tongue over the tip of her tooth and counted his steps until they stopped directly behind her. She could feel the warmth of his breath on her neck.

He was close.

So close.

Too close.

"I asked you a question," he said, his voice low, dangerous.

Serena's breath came in small huffs. She swallowed, feeling a lump growing in her throat and her heart hammered. He was close, that much she knew. But was he close enough to kill? Was he close enough to sink her teeth into his neck and tear out his jugular?

Subconsciously, she took a step back, knocking right into Aaron. She didn't need to see him. She could feel him, the heat of his body radiating off of him. Serena whirled, her nose grazing the prince's as she looked into his cold eyes.

"I wouldn't dare if I were you," he crooned. His lips perked into a smirk and his eyebrows shot up towards his head, as though to silently dare her. *How did he know her thoughts?* Serena's fingers dug deeper into her thumb. *She could kill him. Right here, right now.*

"You're not the first siren I've tangled with, but you will be the last," he cut in, silencing Serena's inner thought.

"What do you mean I'm the last?" she snapped.

"The treaty," is all he replied. Serena turned to face the portrait on the wall.

"You look nothing like her, you know."

"We share eyes, but everything else I get from my father."

"Including his cold, dead heart?" Silence hung in the air and Serena knew she'd hit a nerve. *Finally.*

"Let's just go," Aaron growled. "My father wants to welcome you." A chill ran down Serena's back and her hands began to sweat. Small tremors shook her body as the reality of her situation began to sink in.

She was going to meet her father's murderer.

King Marlow sat tall in his golden throne, his long dark hair falling in curls past his ears. Stubble peppered his shaved chin, casting a five o'clock shadow and atop his head he bore his enchanted golden crown. He appeared no older than forty, though Serena knew the lore. His enchanted crown had warded off the reapers, but she would make sure that death took him into the Underworld. Marlow wore robes of burgundy and vermilion, accented with golden threads and buttons and appeared to shimmer as the light glinted off of them. His jaw was set and his cold, dark eyes were transfixed on Serena. Magic emanated off the king.

Ancient.

Deadly.

At that moment, doubt weighed down on Serena like a ton of bricks. Her feet felt like weights as she followed silently behind Aaron. She looked around the throne room —anywhere but at Marlow—taking in the sights and committing them to memory. Tapestries littered the stone walls and silk scarlet curtains draped between white towering pillars. To her right and her left were rows upon rows of barren feast tables and benches.

Aaron's footfalls ceased as he paused before the dais, halting Serena in her tracks. The prince before her took to his left knee and bowed his head. But Serena would bow to no man.

King Marlow's brow arched, but he said no words as he rose from his throne, his eyes snaking around Serena's curves, taking in her pirate attire.

"Welcome," Marlow's cool voice echoed. Serena remained silent. She would not speak to the man who killed her father and her sister. She would not appease the slayer of her kin.

"Thank you, Father," Aaron replied.

"You may rise." Aaron took to his feet and turned, his eyes flashing with anger as he took in Serena's upright position. Serena flicked her tongue over her tooth and grimaced. She would be chastised later, she was sure.

"Tonight, we celebrate the joining of two kingdoms into one. I have instructed your chambermaids to ready you at once for our ball, and to give you anything you may need. You're not a prisoner here, Serena."

"I beg to differ," Serena snorted, crossing her arms across her chest. "Why are you doing this?"

"Serena!" Aaron snarled. "Mind your tongue."

"Mind yours."

"Enough!" Marlow bellowed. "You two will act as the future of this kingdom or I will make you. Aaron, take your siren bride to her chamber. Now." Silent daggers shot from Aaron's glare as he strode towards Serena, his fingers clasping around her wrist. He squeezed, not hard enough to hurt, but a warning to Serena. No funny business or else. Serena swallowed and gnashed her teeth together. Heavy footfall after heavy footfall, she put King Marlow behind her as the throne room disappeared behind her.

SERENA SAT STRAIGHT UP IN A WOODEN CHAIR, WATCHING the servants fuss with her hair in the shard of glass they called a *mirror*. Her scarlet locks were curled and fastened atop of her head with small golden pins. Two chambermaids attended to her. The servant to her right was a small woman in stature with milky cheeks and golden hair. Her nimble fingers worked eagerly applying makeup to Serena's lids, cheeks and lips. The princess sat transfixed. Watching. Waiting.

She quietly wondered what sort of affair a ball could be. Back home in the Adrellan Courts, they battled for entertainment and counted how many kills they had captured that day by etching the marks into their arms. Their scars were their rewards.

The servant to her left was a rather large woman with ebony hair tossed atop her head in a mop-like fashion. Yellow teeth flecked her smile and her eyes crinkled. She worked hard dabbing white powder onto Serena's cheeks, pluming dust into the air.

"You're going to be so beautiful when we are done with you," she chirped, her voice heavy with her Andoverian accent. Serena coughed, nearly choking on her own saliva as she wheezed for air. She didn't need the fat woman's empty words. She already knew what her looks did to men. She knew how radiant she was and how her prey looked just before she delivered her death blow. She knew how one verse of her song could unravel the strongest of rulers to her beck and call. Serena lowered her head, shooting a glare into the mirror.

She looked so... *human.*

The thought turned her stomach, lurching bile up her throat. She wanted to vomit. She was looking more and more human as the servant girls continued to apply layers of powder to her cheeks, eyes, and color to her lips. Soon, no one would know what she truly was. What sort of *creature* the sea had unleashed upon the land.

Flicking her tongue over her serrated teeth, she felt the familiar prick as blood pooled into her mouth. Her stomach grumbled, sending pangs throughout her body. She needed a distraction. Slowly, she closed her eyes and imagined the ball lined with lifeless bodies as she sank her teeth into each and every carotid artery. Her stomach rumbled again. She imagined the screams that would ring through the air like music to her ears. Every begging courtesan. Serena took in a slow and steady breath before opening her eyes. She cast her gaze away from the mirror and craned her neck to look around the room.

Golden walls shimmered in the candlelight that glowed from nearby sconces. Scarlet velvet curtains hung from large dome-like windows, flowing to the dark wooden floors. A large four-poster bed sat in the middle of the room adorned with white and red flowers.

"The king has gone all out for your arrival. A special guest in our lands. Where did you come from?" the smaller servant asked. Serena looked back into the mirror.

"None of your godsdamned business," she hissed.

"Now, now, miss," Yellow Teeth said, her voice taking on a warning tone. The servant to Serena's right remained quiet, staring back into her eyes through the glass as if she knew the sorts of horrors Serena could bring to Andover.

The girl was young and thin, likely beautiful in human standards, with golden hair as bright as the sun. Her eyes were like large topaz stones, examining Serena as if to get a feel of her *true* intentions. Serena had no intention of letting anyone know what she was up to if she even knew herself. The girl's lips spread from ear to ear as she smiled, but her eyes remained cold and calculating as she busied herself once more.

"Ah," the two women chimed in nearly no time at all.

"You're stunning!" Yellow Teeth beamed. Serena looked at her hair, pinned in intricate curls on her head with flowers of white adorning her crown. She stood, moving towards the dressing curtain and said nothing about her appearance. Her stomach roiled again, wracking pain throughout the siren's body. Serena sucked in a deep breath, fighting against the bile that crept up her throat.

Yellow Teeth followed, her heavy steps echoing across

the floorboards. Serena smiled briefly, imagining the woman falling through the floor. She could hear the wood groan and hiss as the woman's steps neared. Yellow Teeth moved behind Serena and waited. Serena pushed her linen shirt over the top of her head and tossed it to the ground, then slid off her pants and stolen boots.

Yellow Teeth gasped, taking in Serena's naked form as the princess turned to face her.

"You're so thin, miss." She remained silent. Yellow Teeth moved to the chest hidden behind a partition Serena couldn't see from her place in the chair. She watched as the servant grasped a white shell piece. She moved closer to Serena, holding the contraption up to Serena's chest.

"They call this a corset," she said quietly. "All the noble women are wearing them these days. I don't fancy them myself, but…" She moved Serena's hands to her breasts and fashioned behind her as she continued to speak. "Hold it there dear. Now, I want you to take in a deep breath and hold it. I'll count to three. One. Two. Three." Serena sucked in a deep breath as pain erupted from her ribcage. Her ribs felt as though they would crack as Yellow Teeth gave another tug. Serena outstretched her hands, using the curtain to hold herself up. Tears welled in her eyes and rolled freely down her cheeks before she could stop them. Her lungs want to implode and Serena swore her ribs cracked. Why would anyone want to wear such a torture device?

"Marvelous," Yellow Teeth cooed over and over again as she hurried behind the curtain. Serena winced and took a deep breath, hoping the seams would give, but it was no use. She was tied in. She reached back and busied her fingers on the knot the servant had made. Perhaps if she could loosen it, she could get herself free.

"What are ye doing, miss?" Yellow Teeth exclaimed as

she rounded the corner, catching Serena red-handed. "It's customary for royal courtesans to wear a corset."

"Well, is it customary for your royal courtesans to breathe? Because I can't!" Serena shouted. Yellow Teeth's brows rose in surprise and then furrowed.

"Miss, it has to be tight to hold you together."

"I'm not falling apart at the seams!"

"It seems to me that ye are, miss," Yellow Teeth replied quietly. Anger rolled through Serena like a mighty storm. She wasn't a puppet. Not in this land or her own.

"Take this godsdamned contraption off of me," she hissed.

"But, miss—" Yellow Teeth began.

"I don't care. As your future queen, I command it!" Yellow Teeth let out an audible sigh and bustled behind Serena, quietly undoing her corset until the torture device fell free.

"Well, I don't know what's to hold ye together, but at this point, I don't care," Yellow Teeth muttered as she flitted back behind the partition. She returned moments later hugging a large emerald covered dress to her chest. Serena could see layer upon layer of material billow from beneath the skirts.

"You're a lucky lady. The prince had this fashioned for you, made from the best tailors in all of the land."

"Rumor has it that he had the miners dig the best diamonds for this dress," the smaller of the two servants said, rounding the partition. Serena licked at her teeth as irritation built up within her. She was a puppet about to be manipulated by the greatest master of them all, the king.

She didn't care about gems. If the prince wanted to save his kingdom and impress her, he would do best to learn about her or better yet, let her return home.

Fumbling with the material, Yellow Teeth held the dress up for Serena to see.

"It looks like the water when the sun hits it," Serena replied, steadying her voice. Yellow Teeth beamed from ear to ear.

"That it does, miss, that it does! Now, hold up your arms while Leanna and I fashion it over your head." A cool breeze blew through the opened chamber windows, its air pimpling Serena's exposed form, sending a shiver through her body. She'd never been cold before. So instead of arguing, she raised her arms and did as she was told. The two women took a stool on each side of the siren and hoisted the dress over Serena's head.

It fell to the ground with ease and hugged Serena's form. It was snug, yet comfortable, and the skirts that swelled around her waist and legs were soft.

"You look beautiful, miss," Yellow Teeth murmured as she lowered herself from the stool and stepped behind the siren. Craning her neck, Serena watched as the larger chambermaid took two small ties into her hands and began weaving the back of the dress up, tugging every so often.

"Simply beautiful," Leanna whispered from beside the princess, though her gaze said something entirely different. Serena narrowed her eyes, watching with a sidelong glance. She didn't know what she did to the small chambermaid, but she didn't trust Serena and with good reason. She was a monster after all. Serena flexed her jaw, setting it tight.

Leanna did the same.

A *challenge*. Why did she want to challenge her? Serena's mind whirled with the possibilities. Did she work for someone? Or did she want to take the siren princess out herself? Either way, Serena had her eye on the chambermaid, waiting for the first move. Then and only then would she deliver a killing blow to the girl.

"My lady," Leanna said, taking a step forward, eyes locked on Serena, "Are you ready? The king has requested that I accompany you to the ball." A squeak sounded behind Serena as Yellow Teeth sucked a breath.

"You get to attend?" she asked as she walked into Serena's view. "We must get you ready!" But Leanna shook her head.

"No, today is about the lady here. Not me."

"But that's preposterous!" Yellow Teeth stammered. Leanna held up her hand.

"I am to attend as I am. Besides, I really must be going. Mistress Delarose doesn't like me being out long." Serena scrunched her face. So, she *was* working for somebody.

Her mistress. Without a second thought, she cleared her throat and stepped forward, wading on the pads of her feet.

"I'm ready," Serena replied, not allowing Leanna time to speak. Leanna took a step back, closer towards the shadows. Wordlessly, she motioned for Serena to follow as she neared the door. Rolling her eyes, Serena followed, hoisting her skirts high enough to see her feet and tread forward following the servant girl into the hallways.

Light burst from the sconces hanging upon the stone walls, momentarily blinding Serena as she stepped out into the bustling corridors. Silence hung in the air until they neared the ballroom.

Music and laughter greeted her ears. Gold adorned the walls, more gold than Serena had ever seen in her entire life, casually used to decorate the king's castle. She stopped just short of the ballroom, taking in the grandeur of the doors, reaching from floor to ceiling. White marble cooled her bare feet, sending a chill up Serena's spine.

"It's not as scary as it seems," a voice sounded from her side, looping their arm through her own.

Aaron.

Serena's eyes widened as she turned to take in the prince's attire. White and gold swathed him from head to toe aside from the pop of color in his ruby tie. Aaron smiled, flashing the siren his pearly white teeth.

"Do you like my tie?" he asked.

"It's red," she grunted.

"I tried to have it match your hair."

"I see." Serena gritted her teeth. Her stomach knotted and her skin prickled. She'd never been nervous. So why now?

"Shall we?" Aaron asked, motioning towards the large double doors. Bile lurched up the siren's throat, burning her esophagus as she forced it back down with a gulp.

"Um, okay."

"Great," Aaron muttered under his breath before unclasping his arm from hers. He moved with fluid grace and pulled the handle of the large double doors open. The music floating from the room came to a complete halt. Heads turned and eyes bore into Serena as Aaron took to her side once more, wrapping his arm around her waist. Serena did her best to smile, though her insides screamed for her to run. Together they took a step forward and then another. The double doors behind them swung shut, tearing through the silent hall.

"You're late," King Marlow said, standing from his throne, halting them both in their tracks.

AARON

aron's heart hammered in his chest as his father's voice boomed overtop of the crowd. His blood chilled in his veins, halting his legs and Serena at his side. He drew a breath and turned to look at the siren. She stood frozen; her eyes large with what he could only imagine was fear.

"You're late," was all his father said. Aaron gulped down the dread that threatened to take over his body. He knew he was in trouble. He was never to be late to a social event, let alone one in his honor. Clearing the phlegm from his throat, Aaron dipped his chin towards the floor and leaned into a deep bow.

"My humblest apologies, Father," he said between clenched teeth. "I was with our esteemed guest." Heads around them turned as voices echoed through the ballroom, the crowd murmuring at his words.

"Very well," King Marlow grumbled before sitting back in his throne. Aaron stood and let out a relieved sigh, feeling the tension ease from the room. The music resumed to its previous tempo and courtesans took to the dance floor. Turning his attention to Serena, Aaron noted her queasy expression. She was going to have to get over her nerves and the best way to do that was to face them head-on. He held out his hand to her.

"Princess, care for a dance?"

"I don't know how," she admitted, flicking her eyes around the room, focusing on anything but him. Aaron bit at his lip, his heart began to race as he stood looking at her. He had to compose himself, make her think he could do this. Hell, convince himself he could do this.

"Relax, I can teach you." Serena's eyes flickered back to him. She narrowed her eyes and stared at him as though she were searching for answers.

"Fine," she huffed, her fingers curling around his. Her hands were warm and soft to the touch and slightly damp. Aaron drew her close, entwining her fingers within his own. He wrapped his arm around her waist, resting it on the small of her back and drew their furled hands in towards his chest. The princess was close enough to him that he could feel her heart thrumming rapid, erratic beats against his chest. Tilting his head down, he peered into her blue irises and smiled.

"Relax," he murmured again, taking a step forward, swaying in time with the music. Serena followed his lead. Violins erupted through the ballroom, picking up in tempo as Aaron began to move faster. He watched Serena's eyes widen with excitement, keeping his pace. A smile crept onto her face as they stepped in perfect unison, twirling across the dance floor as one. He felt his own smile broaden as he twirled and danced the jig with her.

Something within Aaron cracked, as though a wall he had built between the two of them splintered, letting the siren's light in. There was something about the princess he couldn't place his finger on, a greater good, a kind heart she allowed no one to see. But he would see it. He would believe she was good because if he didn't, he feared her walls would never come down. And what type of marriage would that be? He had to have faith. He had to have trust if he wanted this treaty to work.

Aaron thought of his parents and of their arranged marriage. He thought of his mother's drawn face and faded beauty. His father had sucked the life from her and ruling the kingdom had stripped away her beauty with such stresses. A life he guaranteed she never wanted. A part of him hated his father for forcing him into the same type of situation, but the war had taken so much from Andover and he knew this was for the greater good.

The last note of the violin sang through the ballroom taking Aaron's thoughts with it. Serena looked at him as the king stood, silencing the music once more. He brought a chalice to his perked-up lips and sipped the liquid it contained before smiling wickedly into the crowd.

"Thank you for gathering here this eve as we welcome our prince, Aaron, and the Adrellan princess, Serena to our kingdom. Today we feast and drink. We fornicate and be merry for our prince has returned. But with his return comes a new light for a new tomorrow. It was said that we were doomed if we sailed the Adrellan Pass, that we'd perish at the hands of Poseidon and his kin, but today that changes. Today we signed a Treaty of Peace in exchange for their princess's hand in marriage. And I have to say, that is a great deal." King Marlow sipped from his chalice as the room hung onto his every word. "My boy, Aaron, is hereby betrothed to Princess Serena of Adrella. Long may they reign," he said, holding his glass towards the crowd.

"Long may they reign!" the crowd chanted back. Applause exploded through the room as the court cheered in Aaron's name. King Marlow raised his glass once more, giving his son a silent nod before he took a seat in his throne and began to chat with a spritely young courtesan beside him.

14

CAMILLA

Camilla Delarose could not believe what she heard as wine spewed from her ruby red lips and glass shattered at her feet. Aaron was hers. She was supposed to be marrying him! And now he was marrying some sea wench? Oh, hells no!

Camilla's stomach roiled at the mere thought as she choked on the air in her lungs. She began to cough uncontrollably, sending stabs of pain from her ribs. Hands reached for the lady, helping her to a seat as she gathered her thoughts. Her father, the duke, had bought her marriage with the prince, had handed the king a grand ship worth loads more than their country home and in return, the king had accepted the marriage to his son. Camilla had dreamed of her coronation as queen and could taste the power until it was ripped from her, leaving a hole of desperation.

Tears streamed from her violet eyes, soaking the tips of her black wavy hair. Salty stains trailed down her chest. Her bright blue gown was drenched and Camilla, in a fit of rage, clenched her hands into fists, digging her nails into her palms. She pushed to her feet and set her jaw, her lips placing into a firm line as she set out for the door. She would have her prince if it was the last thing she did.

It hadn't taken long for Camilla to devise a plan after running from the party. Clean air and the sound of waves crashing against the shoreline cleared her mind, paving a path for destruction. She would have her prince. There was no doubt about that. A slight breeze grazed her face as she walked down the beach towards the shipping docks and the very ship named after her. Her tears dried against her cheeks, leaving her skin taut and salty. Crossing her arms across her chest, Camilla's gaze lowered to the ground as another set of sobs overcame her. She dipped her head and pushed her feet into motion, slipping against the sand.

Light spilled down the bank that led to the shipyard as Camilla's angst pushed her up the narrow path leading to the docks straight into something solid and hard. Camilla reached out to grasp something, anything to prevent her fall, but it was no use. Pain radiated up her backside as she hit the ground. Her teeth gnashed together as she bit back her anger and cast her gaze to the object that pile drove her into the ground. Only it wasn't an object, but a person.

Covered in a dark brown colored cloak, the person's face was shadowed.

"My lady, my deepest apologies," the figure's feminine voice replied. Reaching up, the figure lowered their hood.

"Brooksborough?" Camilla sputtered, pushing to her feet.

"Aye. But my lady, please. I truly am sorry." Flicking her tongue over her canines, Camilla smiled. If the pirate was truly sorry, then she could do her bidding. She could kill the siren. Rid her of her problem and win her back the kingdom and the prince's heart.

"Slayer," she crooned, "care to join me in the pub? I have a job for you and the pay will be handsome. Bring trusted friends; you will need them by your side." Silver gleamed from the pirate's side and faster than Camilla imagined, the atmosphere between the two of them changed. The slayer moved, unsheathing a dagger from her hip and extending it towards the lady.

"Is that a threat?" she hissed. "Because one flick of my wrist and my blade will end you. And that's a promise." Camilla gulped, fear coursing through her veins and wondered if she'd made a grave mistake with words.

"You truly dare to threaten me?" Camilla snarled.

"Not at all," Brooksborough led on. "Simply protecting my *ass*-ets."

Regaining her composure, Camilla replied, "Fine. Meet me in the Lower town pub when the moon is still rising. Bring friends. I have a job for you and you won't be sorry." The slayer nodded hesitantly and retreated into the shadows, leaving Camilla alone on the ship docks. Gathering her skirts, she bustled her way into the shadier parts of Andover, the parts she knew the prince would never venture.

Into Lower town.

15

PETAR

"You ruddy 'ole chap." Petar beamed, slinging his arm around Aaron's broad shoulder. Wobbling on his legs, the stench of ale wafted from Petar as he greedily downed another glass. He felt the familiar buzz of alcohol taking its hold on him, coursing through his veins. His vision blurred, giving him double perceptions of his friend whom he now used as a crutch. He could barely hear his friend's laughter over the festivities. Tables and chairs crept into sight and before he knew it, Aaron was placing the drunken pirate down into a seat.

"Stay," the prince commanded, wagging his finger at Petar. The captain blinked, feeling irritation roil within him and sucked in a deep breath. His lungs screamed before letting out the longest yawn Petar had ever mustered. Sleep beckoned him, but here, now, he couldn't give in.

"I may be drunk," Petar slurred, lifting an abandoned glass of ale to his lips, slugging it back, "but I am no dog, Aaron." He slammed the mug onto the table. Silverware and china clinked and clattered, ringing only loud enough for the pair to hear. The double vision of his friend's face hardened and his eyes turned cold.

"Do not make a fool of yourself at my party or I will make you pay," the prince warned. Raising his hands to his face, Petar rubbed at his eyes and leaned forward, resting his elbows on his knees. Petar rose a brow and hardened his exterior as he leaned forward.

"I'll do as I damn please," he slurred, slowly rising to his feet. He watched anger flash through his friend's eyes, but he also knew the prince would not make a spectacle. This conversation was far from over. Aaron turned without another word and silently strode back into the crowd. Reaching out, Petar leaned his hand on the table and watched Aaron return to his siren, taking up dancing with her once more.

The prince was now free from the Delarose's and their unruly reign of terror on his life. He'd removed the claws Camilla had dug into his side and began to stitch up the wounds. Would he be scarred? Perhaps. But, despite the fact he was to marry the siren and sire an heir, Aaron's hardened exterior had begun to melt, slowly but surely.

The prince laughed and joked and drank until his heart was content. He danced the Andoverian dances with the siren princess and as the music slowed into the last song, Petar watched as his friend gently took the siren by her hip and swayed in time with the music. Light glistened off the jewels adorning the princess's gown. She moved closer to Aaron, resting her head against his chest. The look Petar saw in his friend's eyes was something he hadn't seen in a long while.

Happiness. Pure, unadulterated happiness. Petar felt his own lips quirk up, his eyes crinkling in the creases. A smile played on Aaron's lips as he dipped his head into the siren's scarlet locks. Petar closed his eyes, drinking in the sounds around him and the image of Aaron and the siren. He couldn't ruin the moment, not now.

Righting himself, Petar opened his eyes and turned towards the set of large double doors at the entrance of the room, stumbling his way into the corridor.

Aaron was happy. A sentiment he could barely grasp. Camilla had done a number on his friend. Hell, she'd done a number on him, but now, they were all free. Closing his eyes, he took in a deep breath and let out a sigh. He opened his glassy eyes and began his way down hall after hall until he reached a door that let him out to the beach below.

The air was cool against Petar's clammy, sweaty face and the scent of salt and sea greeted his nostrils like an old friend's embrace. A large yellowing moon sat low in the sky, watching over the ocean while casting a white glow onto the water below. Petar chuckled and eyed the waves as they rolled in. He pushed down the bank, his worn boots sinking in the sand with each step, and stopped at the edge of the water. Thrusting his hand into his trouser pocket, Petar felt around for the lone cigarette he'd shoved in there hours before. His fingers curled around the crudely rolled smoke and lifted it to his chapped lips. The taste of stale tobacco greeted the tip of his tongue as Petar's hand fished out his matchbook and flicked it to life. Moments later, the sweet taste devoured his senses, clearing his head.

Petar closed his eyes, inhaling a large drag, feeling the delicious burn in his lungs as the tobacco washed his stress away. He wanted to drift away. Images of mermaids and underwater lands floated through his memory, calming Petar, bringing him peace. The sea was his happy place and always would be.

"I've always loved the sea, too," a familiar voice chirped from his side. Craning a lid open, Petar looked for the owner of the voice he'd heard moan his name the night before.

Mystic. He hadn't heard her approach, which in his state he supposed was a weakness. Pinching his lit smoke between his index and middle finger, his thumb flicked ash into the sand before he raised it to his lips for another taste.

"Care for a smoke?" his gravelly voice asked before letting the smoke filter from his parted lips. He pinched the lit piece and held it out to the siren slayer who smiled, flashing him her ivory teeth, and graciously took the cigarette from him. She lifted the smoke to her own lips and took a long drag of her own.

"I've never been one to settle," he said. "Always coming and going with the tides. My heart aches for the land, to settle down and find a nice gal like yourself and start a family, but my soul belongs to the sea." Mystic chuckled beside him, handing back his smoke.

"I'd hardly say that I constitute as the nice gal type," Mystic replied. Petar remained silent, listening to the music from the party and the waves meld into one song.

"I need to—" Petar started, his words cut off by the female pirate's tone.

"Come with me?" she asked.

"Where?"

"I have a meeting with a client I think you'd very much like to meet. She has coin and drink and jobs. Stay with me. Let me be the moon to your waves." Petar's eyes widened. He wanted to stay, wanted to settle with the slayer and have little pirate children with her. He took in a deep breath and fought against his body begging him to sail. Turning, he faced Mystic and said, "You had me at drink."

PETAR

etar didn't know what they were doing in the slums. He never traveled here. Anything to do with Lowtown meant bad news and everyone knew it. Setting his jaw, his attention was on high alert as the nearby street lamps cast shadows into the dank alleyways leading to the pub. Mystic had said they were going to meet a client and the payout would be worth it in the end, but as Petar's body went rigid, he began to wonder what exactly was at stake.

They moved silent as the night, weaving in and out of alleys, avoiding anyone that ventured out into the street. Blades shimmered in the moonlight from street scum as they scurried like rats; the smell of ale and piss invaded Petar's nostrils and his stomach churned. Music wafted into the roads along with drunkards and barmaids clinging to one another. Unease grew in Petar's gut as they neared the pub and lowering their hoods they entered through the creaky door.

Eyes widened and stares of patrons lingered on them a little too long for Petar's comfort, but Mystic smiled and grabbed his hand, her fingers squeezing his as she led him confidently to a small booth in the back where their client sat.

Dark curls and a familiar blue dress halted the pirate captain in his tracks, yanking the slayer backward. Mystic wheeled on her heels to face him, a grimace playing on her features and released her grip.

He knew their client.

He'd known her for a very long time. Stolen kisses and nights of passion flashed before Petar's eyes as he struggled to keep his sanity in check.

Camilla.

"Come on. Let's go," Mystic said, sidling up in a seat and signaled for Petar to do the same. Heaving a sigh, Petar moved, keeping his gaze low. He shouldn't have come. Everything in him screamed to run back the other way, but his body remained immobile and his blood sent chills through his veins. Guilt knotted in his stomach twisting and forming a hard lump. Aaron would be pissed if he knew where Petar was and who he was with.

"I'm happy to see you obliged," Camilla crooned, latching her gaze onto Petar as she looked him up and down. Hunger and hatred glinted in the lady's eyes. A smirk played on her harlot lips but she remained silent on the matter, keeping to business. *Good*, Petar thought. The sooner they were done, the sooner he would be away from the she-devil and her bags of tricks. Moving slowly, Petar willed his legs forward and slung himself in the seat next to Mystic. He raised a hand in the air, signaling for the barkeep to come take their orders. He needed an ale to get through this meeting and stat.

The slayer leaned forward, clasping her hands together and narrowed her gaze. Around them, the pub roared with life. Patrons sang with the band that played their instruments at a deafening level, loud enough to drown out their conversation to any eavesdroppers. Petar's breath hitched and his heart thrummed with life and regret. He wasn't supposed to be here. He should not have come.

"What is it that you seek?" Mystic asked, her voice snapping the captain from his guilty thoughts. A dangerous question asked to a devious woman. Camilla smiled, playing off innocence Petar knew she was far from, and replied, "Death."

"To whom?" Petar interjected. He hadn't felt the words leave his mouth. Mere thoughts flooded his mind, escaping before he could stop himself. Camilla cocked her head slightly to the side; her smirk grew wider and replied.

"Why, to the siren, of course, my dear captain." Death. Death to the princess and probably Aaron. He had to stop her, but how?

Mystic tensed, her expression souring. He could feel the unspoken emotions radiating off the slayer.

"And what grievance does ye have with the princess?" he asked, offering a reprieve for Mystic. Petar hoped she'd be able to gather herself enough to complete this gathering without bloodshed.

"The little wench stole my crown!" Camilla roared, slamming her fist on the table before standing. Petar slammed his own fist onto the table, eyes from the other pub patrons now on the pair.

"The crown never belonged to a horrid creature like ye! How dare ye speak in vain of our princess!" he seethed, earning a curious sidelong glance from Mystic, who cocked her brow.

"And why would you care about the princess?" Mystic mused. The captain silently sat down, crossing both arms in front of his chest. His own mood turning dark. It was none of their business. This entire meeting was wrong.

"I just care about the state of me mate, 'tis all," he muttered. "I need a godsdamned smoke." Fishing around in his pocket, Petar's fingers fell short and his anxious nerves kept rising. "Oh, mother of pearl," he uttered. "Has anyone got a smoke? I seem to be out."

"Sure thing, Captain," Camilla said, shooting Petar a knowing wink. It was a dirty habit he'd picked up during their nights alone. He remembered the taste of cloves on Camilla's lips as they pushed into his own. The smell of lavender in her hair. The soft slaps of skin against skin. His heart fluttered at the memories as a pang of betrayal shot through him. Petar swallowed and averted his gaze as he reached for the cigarette, lifting it to his lips. The familiar hiss of his matchbook signaled the end of his talk. Three mugs of foaming ale plopped down in front of the group, splashing onto the table as the barkeep scurried away. *Just in time*, Petar thought, grabbing for one. He pinched his cigarette between two fingers and curled his thumb and other remaining fingers around the chilled glass. Camilla smirked, her lips perking in their usual smug fashion and returned her attention back to the slayer.

"So, Slayer, have we a deal?"

"No," Mystic replied, standing up. "We have a bargain, and my price is steep. But we'll discuss it over another round of drinks."

SERENA

*S*erena crashed through her chamber door, beaming from ear to ear. She'd had perhaps the best night of her life. Who would have thought that it would be on land and with their prince? Dancing! She had learned how to dance! And to think the humans had kept this all to themselves! Her smile grew at the thought of her twirling in the prince's arms, at the way her dress skirts billowed out around her feet and the wind in her hair.

Her ears hummed from the deafening music, only to be greeted with silence that the rest of the castle brought. She hummed a tune and turned to shut the door. Inside, her room was cozy. A fire was lit within the hearth and Yellow Teeth bustled about, tidying up as she saw fit. Candlelight flickered from the sconces, casting an orange glow throughout the room. Serena closed her eyes and twirled to her bed, her tune growing louder and louder. Her siren voice begged to sing, but Serena knew that if she unleashed her true voice, her true power, someone would die. And she'd grown rather fond of Yellow Teeth, at least enough to spare her.

"You ought to take a bath, miss," Yellow Teeth muttered as she moved behind Serena. Her fingers quickly worked at the knots of her dress, undoing her gown in mere minutes. The emerald dress fluttered around Serena's feet and she stepped over the fabric. She smiled at the chambermaid and yawned.

"Perhaps tomorrow," she replied, another yawn gripping her.

"Did ye have fun, miss?" Yellow Teeth asked, moving towards the partition.

"I did."

Yellow Teeth peered around the divider and flashed the siren her smile. "Good. Well if ya aren't going to bathe, perhaps ye ought to get ready for bed. Tomorrow is a big day ye know." Serena nodded, fighting off another yawn.

"Okay, but I only want you to tend to me. No more Leanna," Serena said, losing the battle against her yawn. Seeing as she was in no mood to argue, Yellow Teeth simply held her tongue, helping the siren to her wash chamber to wash her face and hair. Serena closed her eyes, letting the maiden do her job and felt a sense of calm wash over her as Yellow Teeth rubbed and rinsed her scalp with fragmented soaps and oils.

"A princess must always look and smell her best." The woman chuckled grabbing for a white plush linen to wrap the siren's hair in.

Sleep beckoned the princess further and dreams of the evening played through her mind.

"Yer all set, miss," Yellow Teeth said, nudging Serena until her eyes fluttered open. "We'll get you in a nightgown and then off to bed with you!" Serena nodded though she wasn't sure what a nightgown was and rose, unashamed with her nakedness. Yellow Teeth didn't seem to notice as she ruffled through drawers, drawing out a white and pink striped cloth. Serena noticed how it resembled the prince's tunic he'd worn when he sailed to get her. Light and airy, made of the same material. The chambermaid held it up, as if to inspect it and muttered, "This will do," before folding it and thrusting it under her arm. Serena stood in the doorway, her head cocked to the side with her eyelids gradually drooping as she watched the strange woman, thinking of nothing in particular.

Yellow Teeth waddled to the siren, her hips swaying from side to side like a ship stuck in a storm. She gestured for Serena to raise up her arms. Serena complied and a moment later the gown fell over her body. Grasping the princess by the crook of her arm, the stumpy chambermaid escorted Serena to her four-poster bed, pulling back the blankets. Serena's limbs moved as her eyes fluttered closed. Sleep gripped the princess, dragging Serena into a dreamless slumber.

SLIVERS OF GOLDEN SUNLIGHT SHONE THROUGH THE windows onto Serena and the floor below. Stifling a yawn, Serena groaned, covering her head with her blankets. Just five more minutes. That was all she needed. But five minutes turned into twenty and before she knew it, Serena had slept an hour. Her eyes snapped open at the realization as Serena pushed up into a sitting position, extending both arms towards the canopy. Her stiff bones popped and cracked and her neck craned from side to side, stretching. She'd never rested better in her entire life. Perhaps life on land wouldn't be so bad, as long as she got to sleep like that, anyway. There was something about today that called to her. Maybe it was waking up in a new realm to a new life that spoke to her or the prospects of a new adventure.

Birds chirped on the ledge of Serena's window, bringing a smile to Serena. She opened her lips and mimicked the whistles of each bird, harmonizing with them. This way, no one would die and her siren voice could be set free. She could feel normal. But Serena knew there was nothing normal about her or her situation. Pushing her blankets aside, Serena rose to her feet, placing each bare sole against the cool wooden floorboards. Her legs quaked as her knees buckled from beneath her, taking the princess by surprise. She supposed the evening's dancing was the culprit for her weak knees, but also that she was new to land. Outstretching her hand, Serena grasped ahold of the bedpost and pulled herself upright. She pushed her legs underneath her once more and ground her teeth against one another as she bit back the dull ache that coursed through her thighs.

Damn these legs. Slowly, she moved towards the windowsill, pushing the curtain aside to look at the world below. Her eyes widened as she took in the colors and the smell. A garden stretched for as far as the eye could see and flitting between the flowers and bushes were faeries. Serena was familiar with the small creatures, having come across them a time or two while finishing a meal. But usually, they left her alone. Their disgusted glances and anxious chirps had always irked the siren, but here, they danced and played and giggled amongst the flowers and greenery.

A brisk breeze filtered the air shuffling Serena's ruby locks and wafted floral scents up to Serena's window. She took a deep breath and relished in the crisp fragrances. She wanted to go to the world below, explore it, live in it. There was so much for her to learn and see. So much for her to discover. A new land called for a new adventure. Then, maybe when her mind was clear, she could focus on her mission. Turning from her ledge, Serena blinked as her eyes adjusted to the shadow cast room and called for her chambermaid. Moments passed and yet she was still alone. Serena scratched her head and furrowed her brow.

"Wench!" she snarled out, using a term she'd learned from the captain. But still, there was nothing. Her tongue flicked over her serrated canines as irritation grew within the siren. Gritting her jaw, she waited a moment longer. When the servant still refused to answer her call, Serena huffed out a sigh and strode towards the door. She would leave her room herself. *Screw Yellow Teeth*, she thought. Her fingers closed around the cool metal knob and she gave it a twist before lurching the heavy wooden door open.

The halls outside the chamber were swathed in natural light that filtered in through the many quartz-stoned pillars that lined the halls. Red and gold silk hung in swags between each pillar and paintings lined the halls. Serena swore there were hundreds of them as an eerie silence filled the air. She hadn't noticed it at first, hadn't noticed the lack of souls bustling about the corridors, and that didn't sit well with the siren. Something was going on. If something devious was taking foot on the castle grounds, she wanted to be as far away from it as possible. Fewer chances that anyone could pin her for the misdeed if she was far faraway. Shaking her head, Serena pushed the nagging thoughts of doom aside and focused on exploring the gardens below. She wanted to feel the lush greenery beneath her feet, squish it between her toes.

The sun settled high in the sky as Serena weaved from hall to hall until she found her way to the gardens. Flowers bloomed all around her, in every shade imaginable. Her lips perked and a genuine smile spread across the young princess's face. She'd never seen anything so beautiful in all of her life. A single tear pricked from her eye, rolling down her cheek as Serena brushed it away. She'd never felt a tear either. This human life of hers was… *beautiful*. And the more Serena thought about her new life, the more tears rained down her cheeks until she crumpled into a sobbing heap on the sod below. Her fingers brushed every blade of luscious green grass, noting how stiff and yet soft it was when a flutter of wings ripped through the air. Serena sniffed back her blubbering and wiped the tears from her eyes before looking around.

Pixies.

With white and silver wings, the small creatures flitted from flower to flower, gathering drops of dew in their arms before hurdling them at one another. Laughter broke out from the pixies in high frequencies that Serena was sure only she and other creatures could hear. But it made her giggle, nonetheless. The little people continued to gather dewdrops and threw them at one another while the princess rose to her feet and wandered.

Off ahead in the distance, the sound of water called to her siren soul. It felt like ages since she'd touched the water, though she knew it had only been a full day. If only she could dip her toes in…

She moved with grace, letting the water call to her, letting the laughter and flutter of pixie wings drown out any ill thoughts until the crash of water upon water filled her ears. A small waterfall fed into a pond of crystal and there, lounging on the banks were nymphs. Some brushed at their hair while others lounged around and poked at the water.

Cousins. As if the nymphs could hear her thoughts, their heads snapped up and turned their attention to the princess. Serena's eyes widened as she cleared her throat and took a step forward, looking into their glassy black eyes. The nymphs blinked but said nothing.

"Hello, cousins," Serena greeted. But the nymphs

merely blinked in response before they all hissed, "*Sssssiren.*"

"Yes. Siren," she repeated before taking another step towards them. Each nymph narrowed their beady eyes, acting as though they were one and the same, operating as a whole.

"We are no cousin to evil. Blood stains your hands, evil runs through your veins. You have no business in these parts of the castle. You have no business where good reigns." The nymph's words cut deep, slicing her to the core. Serena's body froze. She wasn't all bad. She was learning to be good, to have patience, but that would take time. Right? *Right?* Serena opened her mouth to speak, but no words escaped her parted lips. The nymphs smiled coyly and scattered like droplets of rain into the water.

They hated her. They *all* hated her.

She would be alone forever in this world above the sea.

No friends.

No family.

A prince that hated her and a kingdom that didn't trust her.

Serena dropped to her knees, pain erupted through both of her kneecaps, but she didn't care. Her life would be pain and then she would die. Die a lonely death with no one to mourn her, no one who cared. Tears brimmed her ocean blue eyes, spilling as they cascaded down her cheeks. A sob caught in her throat and the siren crumbled from within.

Hours had passed as the sun dipped below the horizon, painting reds, oranges, and purples across the clouded sky. Serena hadn't moved a wink, taking in the garden and pixies and digesting the fact that the castle held water nymphs. Digesting the fact that she would be alone. Forever. Their hisses had hurt feelings she'd never expressed. Silent tears continued to fall freely from her lashes as she sat at the water's edge, trailing her index finger through the surface. Her thin nightgown did little to warm her, but she didn't care. Serena was numb. Absently, she watched scales form and disappear as she withdrew her finger from the water. She remained like that for some time, before huffing a breath and getting to her feet. One thing had always comforted the princess. Slowly, she reached for her nightgown, her fingers curling around the rim of the fabric before hoisting it up and over her head. The crisp air bit at her exposed skin, pebbling it as her hairs stood on end. Serena discarded the cloth on the ground behind her and dove into the pond below.

A chill of delight and adrenaline coursed through the princess's veins, as she glided further down. Serena opened her eyes, realizing that she had shut them when she jumped and looked around. Blue light emanated around her body, illuminating the water around her, swathing her. Scales peppered Serena's arms, green and shimmering as her legs began to knit together with black thread. Hot stabbing pain erupted from the stitches, burning Serena as the sensation engulfed her body. Purple blood pooled from her wounds; Serena opened her mouth to scream, but no sound escaped her parted lips. Water rushed into her lungs, choking out the air as she transformed. Serena clutched at her neck, flailing her arms to hurdle towards the surface, but her body remained motionless. The siren's eyes widened as the realization hit her. She was going to die before the transformation was complete. Darkness coated her vision, tunneling it as fear gripped Serena and the world around her faded to black.

PETAR

$\mathcal{P}$etar clutched at his throbbing head wondering how he'd managed to make it back to his room after spending the rest of the night down in the Lower town pubs with the she-devil, Camilla, and Mystic. His eyelids dropped, blocking out the sun that shone through the halls leading out into the gardens. He needed quiet and time to think… about everything. Had he betrayed Aaron? He didn't know. But he knew he needed to get out of sight and go to the one place in the entire castle that would calm his raging hangover. The gardens had always held a special place in the captain's heart. Peaceful and quiet. It was a place he had always visited when he was in Andover. He had to visit Tink after all.

The small pixie had once saved his life after he washed up on the Andoverian shores as a wee boy. Petar gulped at the memory and sucked in a deep breath as he pushed the frightful occurrence to the back of his mind. Thinking of Tink always brought a whirlwind of emotions to the pirate. She was grace and fury wrapped in a tiny husk of a human with silvery-white wings that glittered in the sunlight. Her tiny handmade dresses made from the earth brought a smile to his lips and her pointed ears that curved towards the sun reminded him that this cold world he lived in still held its magical secrets. He adored Tink, his very first friend.

Before he knew it, Petar was at the gardens entrance and a sense of calm washed over him. He picked at a nearby red thorn rose, before calling out.

"Tink? Tinkerb—" Petar blinked as his pixie whizzed into view. Her sandy locks a mess and her home-sewn leaf dress fraying at the seams.

"Get it together," he muttered under his breath as the pixie landed on his shoulder. She spoke rapidly in tongues the pirate had learned long ago, in a language long forgotten. Petar's eyes widened as his blood chilled in his veins.

"What do ye mean the siren's 'ere? Thought she'd be with Aaron today." His gaze flashed to Tink and his body tensed.

"No? What? Drowning? Nymphs! Show me the way, Tink!" Pushing his legs forward, Petar ran. Bile rose in his stomach, stinging his throat as he pushed the vomit down. Pain radiated in his side, but he continued onward. He ran until his lungs burned and his legs yearned for him to stop.

But he couldn't stop.

Not until he reached her. The sound of water babbling grew closer, greeting him like an old friend. The waterfall came into view and Petar pushed his legs into overdrive. Without hesitation, Petar lunged from the bank, catapulting himself into the pond.

He *couldn't* let Serena die.

He *wouldn't* let her die.

The freezing water pricked his skin and he could feel the change coming but pushed further into the depths. He knew ascending was unavoidable, but he pushed through the pain. Spotting rays of baby blue, Petar swam faster, his lungs burned as the unconscious princess came into sight; her body drifting towards the dark floor. Petar gritted his teeth as his arms scaled and his own legs knit together with black threads, scaling in deep hues of emerald.

Stabbing pain coursed through the captain's legs as his own dark purple blood seeped from his stitches. But he didn't care. He had to save her. Swimming as fast as his body would allow, he reached the princess and curled his fingers around her wrist, hauling her up into his arms. For a moment, the pair drifted down into the depths before a screech tore from the captain's throat—feral and familiar. Petar knew he had fully changed. His eyes shifted, untouched by the watery depths and focused on the life around them, on the nymphs and their giggles as they watched the princess drown. Breaking into a haunting melody, they taunted Petar.

> *Down, down, down they go.*
> *Where they'll die*
> *We all will know.*
> *Down, down, to Hades they seek*
> *Down, down they all will creep.*

Creations, Petar thought and unleashed an otherworldly screech. The nymph's song stopped; all eyes were on him.

"If you touch the princess again, I will end you," he hissed in a tongue long neglected. "If you touch my *sister* again, there will be no gods for you to pray to. No afterlife for you to frolic in. If you harm her, I will kill you." Petar knew his words hit home as he watched the nymphs snarl in his direction. The princess's body grew heavier with each passing moment. Heaving a breath, Petar wrapped one arm under her knees and the other around her waist and swam towards the surface.

Hues of blue and black painted the sky as the sun set below the horizon. The evening's air brought the slightest breeze, nipping at Petar's skin as he breached the surface, hurling the siren onto the bank. Pain erupted through his body, tearing screams from his lungs as he shifted once more.

The chilled air barely affected the captain's now naked form, his clothes torn to shreds during the transition as familiar wings fluttered next to his ear and tiny feet landed on his shoulder. A sigh rippled through Petar as he turned to face his friend.

"Tink, can you sheathe me just this once with your pixie dust?" Silence greeted him, but Petar knew that that the answer was yes when the scent of lemons and strawberry filled his nostrils. Dust coated his bare body, transforming into fabric before his eyes. Within seconds, the pirate was cloaked in clothing made from magic.

"Thank you Tink, yer the best," he replied. Tink giggled and placed the smallest of kisses upon his cheek before flying away. Turning his attention back to his sister, Petar knelt.

The siren's lips were blue as Petar hovered over top of Serena, sucking in a deep breath before giving her a breath of life. He watched her chest rise and fall, but her body remained limp and motionless. Dread coursed through his veins. He couldn't let her die. Not for the sake of the kingdom. For Aaron... He sucked in another breath and pushed it into her lungs.

"Come on," he gritted out through clenched teeth. Weaving his fingers between one another, Petar placed his palm over the top of his right hand pushing on the princess's chest. His arms screamed with agony and bones crunched beneath him. "Come on! Come on!" he cried out, pushing another breath into the lifeless siren. How would he explain it to Aaron? What would become of the two kingdoms? War and bloodshed played like a slideshow in the captain's head when a small cough came from the siren's throat and her body lurched forward.

A jolt ran through the captain's body and on instinct alone he hauled the siren upright. Water poured from her mouth, enough that death surely was on her doorstep. The princess opened her left eye and cast Petar a sidelong glance.

"You smell like my enemy," she croaked out. Petar grinned and thrust his fingers into his pockets, retrieving a cigarette and lifted it to his lips. If only she truly knew.

"We have much to discuss, Princess," he replied and pulled her back into his arms. Her eyes slid closed as her head rested against Petar's chest. Although he thought that she would have given him more of a fight for touching her, she slid into a slumber as he hoisted her into his arms and the pair headed back into the castle.

19

SERENA

Serena startled from her dreamless slumber as a knock sounded on her door. She didn't remember coming back to her chamber after being out in the gardens. She remembered the pond and… *Gods!*—drowning. Her muscles ached and nearly seized as she pushed herself to sit up. Swinging her legs around, the princess attempted to stand. Her knees quaked and buckled beneath the siren and she hit the wooden floor with a *crack*. Pain flared from her backside up into her back and a small cry escaped her lips. Wrapping her fingers within the bed linens, Serena hauled herself upright and back onto the bed.

"Come in," she rasped out. Her vocal cords stung from the near-death experience. She could still taste the pond water in her mouth, could feel it choking out the air from her lungs. A hand raised to her head before sliding down to rub her face. It was all a dream. A horrible, horrible dream…

The thick chamber door swung open, creaking on its hinges exposing the captain on the other side, leaning against the frame with a cigarette placed between his chapped lips. Thick grey smoke flowed from the tip, a bitter and sweet smell filled the room. Serena narrowed her gaze, wondering what he could possibly want with her. But before she could ask, Petar pushed from the wall and strode in.

"Put that nasty thing out," Serena hissed, pinching her nose with her thumb and forefinger. "And tell me what you want." Bile rose within her throat as the captain puffed again on the cigarette before peeling it from his lips.

"We have much to discuss," was all he said.

"Care to elaborate? Or do you keep all of your conversations aloof? To what do I owe this visit, Captain?" The captain let out a groan, his lips pressing into a hard line and threw himself down next to her on the bed, jostling Serena.

"How long was I out?" she asked.

"Five days."

"Five days!" Serena tensed. Five days frozen unconscious in a foreign land, defenseless. Five days for them to do whatever they wanted to her.

"I came to give ye a message, me lady," the captain continued. Serena's eyes darted from the man on her bed to the open door and back. Servants passed in the hall, casting occasional glances before dipping their chins to their chests and quickening their pace. If word was out that the prince's betrothed was in bed with another man, let alone the prince's best friend, what would the kingdom think? What would they do? Hell, what would the prince do? Serena didn't care to find out.

Taking in a deep breath, Serena got to her wobbling legs and took a step towards the door. Her knees visibly shook and before she could hit the floor, an arm was cloaked around her, hauling her upright. She was weak. So damn weak in this husk of a body. She was growing tired of falling, of being like a new foal, trying to learn how to walk. She was fierce and feared when she was in the water. But on land? Not so much.

"Easy there," Petar crooned, helping Serena back to her cooling spot on the bed. He turned and closed the door, listening as the latch clasped behind him before whirling to face Serena. Silence hung in the air before Serena cleared her throat and croaked, "It's very inappropriate for a man to be in my chambers." She could feel Petar's eyes on her, studying her. If he made a move on her, she would kill him or at the very least, *try*. It had been some time since she'd had a proper siren meal and for a moment a shudder ran through her body at the prospect of eating a man. What was happening to her?

"Aye," Petar replied, clasping his eyes shut, shaking his head. "It would be inappropriate if I came here with other intentions in mind, me lady." Serena glimpsed a sidelong glance at the captain before adjusting herself to face him.

"And you don't?"

"Hardly."

Serena sucked in a breath. "Very well then. To what do I owe your nightly company?" The pirate shifted uncomfortably as if her question picked at a festering wound. Moments passed and Serena grew weary and irritated before the captain slowly answered.

"The slayer is planning on betraying you." His voice was low as if the walls had ears and their conversation would soon be the talk of the town.

The princess's eyes widened. "And why are you telling me this?" she asked. "I thought you and the slayer were in each other's company?" She smirked at the last word. Company was putting it mildly. The pair were an item at best and a deadly one. The pirate shifted again, meeting her gaze with urgent intensity.

"Because I like you," he replied.

"Enough to betray her?" Her question was genuine. Did he like her enough to betray his consort? The captain shook his head and pinched the bridge of his nose with his thumb and index finger while casting his gaze towards the floor.

"That's not what I meant," he replied.

"Then get to it," she growled.

"We are alike, you and me. Like rum to a pirate, we share a connection. When I look at ye, well…" he hesitated, "I see me." Serena flicked her tongue over her teeth as she tried to decipher the pirate's nonsense. Her jaw clenched, and she fought the irritation that continued to bubble within her and replied, "In what ways? You are a man and I am not. You are a human and I am not. Andover is your home, not mine. I am a long way from Adrella. You, on the other hand, are free to go as you wish, whereas I am free to roam these halls. We are nothing alike. You are free and I am a prisoner sentenced to death." Another long pause swelled between the pair, tension rising with each passing second.

"We are both children of the sea," Petar replied. Serena pursed her lips, wondering where the conversation was turning, but Petar continued parting his lips. Then he began to sing.

"Come with me and then you'll see, For a child of the sea is what I was born to be." A song she knew so well. A melody that shook the princess to her core. "Tell me, Princess, why do you think I live my days upon a ship?" Serena remained silent, but she knew. Knew what he was. Had smelled it upon him as she awoke from her nightmare.

Siren.

Petar continued, "I was barely a boy when my mother was killed in the war. Alone in the seas and cast out by my own kind, I stumbled to shore with the waves and endured my first ascension. I was five at the time. My body broke and I nearly died. And honestly, I had wanted to. I hoped I would join my mother, but I did not join her soul in the afterlife. I was not chosen by the gods to have that honor. The Fates showed me no mercy as I stood on that beach, broken, naked and alone at such a feeble age. Instead, I was found by a captain and his rowdy crew of lost boys and taken aboard a ship, my home, my true home.

"Hook knew what I was. He and his maiden, Wendlynn, raised me on the seas. We landed in Andover where I met the pixies, where I met Tink. You can thank her ye know when ye see her. She's the one who saved yer life. Anyhoo, Hook and Wendlynn settled in Andover after sailing the seas for five long years. I was ten at the time. When they found themselves working fer the king, they never told him what I was. Never wanted me to fear fer me life, so they took me secret to their graves. Me father's last words, Hook's last words, to me were to follow me heart." Serena eyed him suspiciously, before hearing Petar speak the words the ocean knew.

"My heart lies with Adrella."

"And your loyalty?" Serena pushed.

"Me loyalty will always be with Andover," he hesitated. "You are me princess and me sister. Poseidon sired us both. And right now, I'm trying to save yer life. The slayer is planning a coup d'état with Camilla Delarose."

"What is it they plan to do?" she nearly whispered. Bile lurched in the princess's throat as her stomach knotted. Her mind whirled trying to digest the information thrown at her. Raising a hand to her mouth, the princess burped, fighting back the vomit that threatened to escape and sucked in a deep breath.

"To take the thing that is dearest to you."

"They can't take Adrella," she countered. "Aramis would never allow it."

"But they can take your voice." Her voice. Her means of defense. Her ability to rule. They could destroy her, kill her. And for what? Serena's heart hammered against her ribcage as she fought to catch her breath. She couldn't think, couldn't breathe.

"I won't let them," Petar said, his voice taking on a calm tone. "To take your voice, they would have to find the sea witch."

"Ursulana. But she is a legend. A story we tell our guppy kin to make them act right," Serena started.

"She is very much real, Princess. She can be found when there is something in it for her."

"A life for a life. Perhaps Camilla plans on sacrificing the slayer in return for my downfall?" Serena asked.

"That won't happen. Ursulana doesn't touch family."

"Family? How is the slayer family?" Petar smiled, flashing Serena his pearly white teeth.

"She's not. But the child within her carries siren blood. That is her only saving grace." Candles flickered, casting shadows across the room as Petar quietly opened Serena's chamber door. "*Reat atu*," he said, rest up, in Adrellan. "Tomorrow we fight for Adrella." Petar exited the chamber, leaving Serena alone with her thoughts.

PART II

Two strangers join as one
Two strangers, a night of fun.
Within their passion, magic grows,
To a creature unseen and no one knows.

20

MYSTIC

*M*ystic knew about the *bump* growing along with her belly, though she was unsure when she had conceived or who the father was. She had been sharing the bed with the prince's captain, but she'd shared beds with many captains and drunken patrons since being dismissed by the prince from her royal duties. If he didn't want her expertise and protection, then so be it. Not many days had passed since she'd shared a sleepless night with Petar, though magic had a funny way of working in Andover. Home to faeries and mythical beasts, magic reigned in Andover long before she'd even set foot on the ancient land. And magic had found its way into her womb.

Slugging back another pint of goat's milk, wishing it were ale, Mystic fought back the urge to vomit the contents of her stomach onto the pub floor. Bile lurched up her throat as she doubled over, wrapping both arms around the creature that grew within her. Sharp knotting pain twisted in her belly and tears peppered the slayer's eyes, running in silent streams down her cocoa complexion as she ralphed below.

She hated this.

Hated the *thing* that grew within her.

Hated the ball and chain that would keep her in this wretched land.

Mystic drew in a slow breath, bracing her hands on her knees and focused. She could do this. She had a mission that depended on her and she would be damned if she let this *thing* stop her. She drew another breath, wincing slightly as the sharp pains began to recede.

She had to find the sea witch and tear the siren's voice from her throat before she enchanted Andover. Without her voice, the princess would be defenseless. Without her voice, she could slay the beast. Something she was rather good at and her mistress could return to her rightful spot alongside the prince.

Mystic smiled as she thought about all the gold she would be awarded. She could finally buy her own ship and sail the seas until her last breath, but then she remembered her *creature* and her mood turned sour. She was not the mothering type. Hades, she didn't even know if she could muster up a caring gene in her body.

She'd known bloodshed from a young age after being taken in by the infamous former siren slayer, Kirkwell Blackbeard. A man known for his brutality and swift kills. The same man who showered her in weapons and congratulated her when she slew her first siren. How would she take care of a child?

Her stomach roiled again at the thought. Swallowing the lump that had formed in her throat, Mystic shook the rapid thoughts from her mind. She would deal with the creature when the time came. Whenever the time came. The slayer's eyes fluttered shut as she took in a clarifying, calming breath and refocused back on her task.

She and Camilla had devised the plan after long deliberation in the pub that night with Petar, when he'd sworn to help her find the sea witch, claiming he knew just how to summon the forbidden beast from the depths of a watery hell.

Mystic was grateful for him. As the pain subsided, she stood, sweat pouring from her brow, and set out into the night. Darkness greeted the slayer as she raised the hood of her cloak and set off into the slums. The cool evening air nipped at her drenched flesh, sending a shiver down her spine. Buildings sat nearly atop one another, painted in shades of pink, whites, and yellows. The cobbled streets catching on her slippered feet. She moved silently, deadly, weaving in and out of alleys as she headed towards the port. No soul dared to be out this late when the moon hung high in the midnight sky. She would find a crew and a ship.

Then she would set sail.

Weaving in and out of alley after alley, Mystic recalled the letters she'd written to Petar that morning. She asked him to meet her at the docks, but she knew it would be a slight chance. He wasn't as enthusiastic about their meeting with Camilla like she had been. Mystic wondered if she'd made a grave error in judgment. Could she trust him? She hadn't received word back. Doubt lingered in her mind. Would he show up? Or would he leave her to figure things out for herself?

Gritting her teeth, Mystic dipped into another alleyway, disappearing into the shadows. The scent of salt and fish infiltrated her nostrils, letting the slayer know she was close. The sea was near and it sang to her soul. Moving so that her feet were heel to toe, Mystic made no sound as she entered a clearing to the edge of the harbor.

Ships littered the port, some large and grand, some

small and quaint, used for fishing, but one, in particular, caught the slayer's eye.

The Camilla Rose.

The prince had humiliated her in front of everyone and now, it was her time for justice. Small as it may be, Mystic's lips curled as she thought of the prince without his vessel.

"Don't even think about it," a male voice warned from behind.

Petar.

He had shown up after all. Thank the gods.

"And here I was thinking you wouldn't show."

"I wasn't going to," he admitted, "but then I saw ye eyeing up me ship and thought that if I were an outcast pirate, paid to do a job that the crown prince's ex commissioned, where would I go? First, I would take his ship and then I would take his crew. The answer was clear and predictable." He shrugged.

Mystic ground her teeth together to keep from seething. She still didn't know if she could trust Petar, but she did know he knew her plan and well enough to predict her next move. Her tongue flicked over her teeth as she fought against her irritation. She closed her eyes, craning her neck this way and that until small pops of her joints broke the awkward silence between the pair.

"Fine. Yes. I was going to take the ship. We have a mission and we need a crew. What else was I to do?"

"Buy one? Not commit a crime against the crown!"

"With what gold?" Mystic hissed. "Mine stopped coming when that prince of yours fired me in the harbor before the town."

"You were going to kill his bride!"

"I was trying to save his life!" Mystic snapped. Waves crashing against the shoreline was the only sound to break the silence for several moments before Mystic turned and said, "I'm taking *the Camilla Rose*."

"No, yer not."

"Yes, I damn well am. If you want to see your precious ship unharmed, then come with me." Who was he to tell her what she could and could not do? She was the gods-damned siren slayer! Heir of Kirkwell Blackbeard. Her words were final. The captain's brows drew together as his jaw hardened.

"Fine," he ground out.

"Splendid," Camilla's shrill voice said from behind them. Mystic's hair rose on end. The mistress was frightening and strong and there was something about her that the slayer appreciated. Perhaps it was the way she took what she wanted and didn't let anyone get in her way. Or perhaps it was her cunningness.

Mystic turned to face Camilla Delarose, the strongest woman—besides herself of course—to walk on land. Her lips curled into a smirk as she took in the marquess's attire. Even on a mission, she was dressed to the nines. Camilla stood with her arms crossed across her chest, her manicured nails tapping along her crossed arms. She sported a violet gown made of Alcoveran silk that fell to the ground, the ends wet from the dew. A darker purple cloak covered her shoulders from the chilly air and her dark curly locks ran down her back.

"Mistress, what are you doing here?" the slayer asked.

"Making sure that our arrangement follows through," Camilla replied, clucking her tongue before walking over to the captain, looping her arm through his. "Shall we?"

"We still need a crew," Petar replied as his baritone voice cut through the night.

"I've secured a ship and a crew," Camilla said,

gesturing towards a large mahogany ship that sat a few down from the prince's.

"Mistress," Mystic whispered. Camilla turned, flashing a sneer to the slayer as she looped her arm around Petar's.

"Yes, well, I've arranged a crew for us already," Camilla replied. "Shall we?" she asked gesturing towards a large mahogany ship. Mystic's eyes widened; she hadn't paid attention to the smaller ship. But it was grand and would do for the journey.

With a wink, Camilla released Petar's arm, patting gently before waltzing past the slayer towards the docked ship; her skirts billowing behind her.

Mystic turned to Petar. "She can't come with us. It's a death wish!" Petar's lips smiled weakly as he shrugged.

"Let her come," was all he said, before following on Camilla's heels.

MYSTIC

*W*ater sprayed over the ship's side as they sailed through Adrellan waters. Mystic stood with her damp clothes clinging to her body, looking out into the distance. This plan was insane. Camilla was insane! But this was really happening. They were searching for the sea witch, a creature so bold, so powerful and mischievous that even Hades would not welcome her into the Underworld. Mystic closed her eyes and sucked in a deep breath, trying to calm her nerves. If she wasn't so desperate for coin, she'd never have taken the job. But desperate times called for desperate measures.

Deadlier than the gorgons, the sea witch was said to shift with the tides, morphing into whatever creature she pleased to avoid being detected. How they were supposed to find her was beyond Mystic.

Petar had said he knew how, but Mystic was sure he only said it to impress her. Instead, he'd impressed the wrong woman. She couldn't be mad at him either. It was her own damn fault for landing them here. She'd been the one to make a deal with the devil. Wiping beads of sweat and spray from her brow, Mystic watched as the sun crept up over the horizon, spilling rays of orange, red, and yellow across the sky in a medley of warmth.

She hadn't slept a wink, hadn't even claimed a bunk in the decks below. Instead, she'd spent the night second-guessing herself. She needed a damn ale, and maybe a smoke, too. So much depended on her. If she failed, there would be a monster on the throne. Hell, if she won, there'd be a monster on the throne. At least she'd be human though.

Mystic closed her cocoa lids and braced both hands against the ship's cool wooden side. Calloused fingers glided around her own, weaving themselves in between one another. Warmth filled her hand. Mystic's lips perked into what she knew was a weak smile as she turned to Petar. Wind whipped his sandy hair and he squinted his eyes, looking out at the horizon.

"It's going to be okay," he said, though she hadn't said anything at all. "Yer going to be a great mum." His words hung between them, sucking the air from Mystic's lungs. Her body tensed and then froze. He *knew*. How?

"But—" she choked out before a hard lump cut the words from the slayer's throat.

"We 'ave so much to talk about," Petar said, giving her chocolate fingers a reassuring squeeze. Turning, Petar's eyes met her own. "In due time. Until then, we have until the sun hangs high in the sky to reach the west of the Pass. Then we can begin the call for the sea witch." Mystic nodded. Suddenly, everything felt heavy. She leaned over and rested her head upon the pirate's shoulder and together, they watched the sunrise.

Hours passed as the ship rose and fell with the waves. Mystic hadn't moved, but instead, fixated her eyes out into the blend of nothing. Waves and rock surrounded them as the ship crossed through the arched Pass of Adrella and somewhere in the dark shadowy depths was the sea witch. For all she knew, the witch could be watching them right now.

Petar stood at the captain's wheel shouting orders to the crew. Feet clambered around her and hairy arms pushed and nudged her body this way and that. The ship hung a hard left, merely inches from the dark rocky sides. Pebbles skittered onto the deck behind her causing Mystic to jump. She moved, clutching her head, moving for the first time in hours. Her limbs had grown stiff, sending a dull ache through them. Mystic closed her eyes and rubbed her palms over her face watching the Pass open up into a calmer, darker place.

An eerie silence enveloped them. This was definitely not a place for sailors. This was death. Mystic moved closer to the side and peered overboard into the black sheet of water below. No reflection shone back at her. There was nothing but still darkness. A chill ran down her spine, sending shudders through the slayer's body and the hair on the back of her neck raised.

The ship's speed slowed to a crawl and Petar moved, taking up a spot along the railing next to Mystic. He cleared his throat, parted his lips, and then began to sing. His voice was low and eerie, quieting everyone aboard the ship. Mystic watched men around her begin to stiffen and felt her own body do the same.

Magic has a price to pay.
Of blood and sin, we all could say.
Nothing in this realm is free.

Come to me, a witch of the sea.
I seek a favor none can grant.
With blood, I give but know I shant.
You have my word, my song I give.
For none alone have ever lived.

Gurgling sounded from below, shaking the ship. Bubbles rolled around the ship like a pot on boil. Men shouted, grabbing onto anything they could. Mystic's eyes widened with surprise. Magic. Pure, raw magic. The ship shook again, hard, knocking the slayer to her knees. She winced as her knees cracked against the floorboards, sending waves of hot pain through her legs. She grabbed the ship's side, hauling herself upright before she whirled back on Petar.

A smug smile glimpsed his lips. The ship shifted hard to the right, nearly knocking the slayer to her knees again. She winced, digging her nails into the wood, but Petar remained motionless, waiting. Crew members began shouting, taking cover in the decks below, until the slayer, the captain, and Camilla were the only ones who remained.

Wood groaned beneath the slayer's feet as a shock wave lurched the ship hard again. She feared sinking, fear that Petar had made a grave mistake and dug her aching nails deeper into the wood as she held on for dear life. Petar stood with his arms crossed and a beaming smile on his face. Then, the water below began to settle. Bubbles popped leaving the surface like a sheet of glass. The air around them chilled, becoming eerily quiet once more.

She was coming. Whatever she was.

The baby within Mystic moved, kicking her in the ribs. It was impossible, she'd just found out she was pregnant. But then again, magic was at work here and anything was possible when it came to magic.

As if on cue, the ship lurched hard before four black and purple tentacles rose from the depths, tearing at the ship's side. The scream in Mystic's throat died. Fear and adrenaline coursed through her vein as she rested her hand upon the hilt of her siren's blade. Ear-piercing screams flooded the air as tears rolled down Camilla's cheeks. Tentacles moved, suctioning onto her milky flesh as more legs hauled themselves overboard. Releasing the ship's side, Mystic sucked in a deep breath and drew her blade.

She lunged, slicing down hard on the tentacle, cutting it straight through. Her legs moved faster than her mind, running to the heiress. Camilla sat with her knees bent to either side of her, sobbing as her fingers clutched at the suction cups fastened tightly to her arms. Mystic knelt, pulling a dagger from her hip and pried at the tentacle. Slowly, cup after cup began to loosen, but there was no more time to spend. The ship jerked again.

"Go below deck," Mystic whispered. Camilla nodded, rubbing at her purpling hand.

"Th-thank y-you," she blubbered out. Mystic stood, extending her hand to the marquess, hauling her to her feet. Camilla moved quickly to the stairs.

The slayer remained still, watching until the marquess descended before focusing her attention back on the beast and Petar. Mystic whirled to face the large octopus-like creature that sloshed and jostled before them, consumed in purple light. The light grew brighter and brighter, nearly blinding the slayer. Mystic squinted, watching as the creature before her transformed. The light before her dimmed until there was nothing left.

"Ursulana," Petar cooed, dipping low into a bow. The creature before them was nearly human, except for the pale blue skin. She wore an ebony dress, adorned with dark purple gems. The dress clung to the witch's every curve with a sweetheart neckline that dipped low enough to expose her breasts. White hair fell in waves down to her shoulders and her violet eyes were striking as they bore into the pair.

"Which of you sliced the tip of my tentacle off?" Ursulana sneered, her tone dripping with a toxic hatred. Every fiber in Mystic froze, watching as the witch's eyes narrowed onto her. Her breath quickened and her heart hammered against her chest. She was going to die.

"You reek of my blood," the witch hissed, dropping her gaze to Mystic's siren's blade, and she slowly walked towards Mystic. "You're lucky that I will regenerate when I return to the sea. And-" she hesitated, turning to face Petar, "that his blood runs through your child's veins."

Mystic couldn't breathe. As she opened her mouth to speak, Ursulana whirled and faced Petar.

"You dare summon me?" she spat.

"Aunt Ursu-" Petar began, but the sea witch held up her hand, silencing the words from his tongue. Mystic's eyes widened. *Did he call her aunt?*

"Nothing in this world is free," she sang back to the captain and narrowed her eyes. "With blood, you give and the wish I grant. Where is my sacrifice?"

Sacrifice?

"Well, about that," Petar mumbled, shuffling his feet. He lowered his gaze.

"I do nothing for free, boy!" the sea witch bellowed. "I want my sacrifice or I leave!" Petar raised his head, meeting the beast's eyes.

"She's below deck," he muttered. *Gods no. Please no.* Mystic's stomach knotted and her eyes widened as she realized who the sacrifice was. The crew was all male and the only other female was—

"You can't. She's an innocent. Camilla has nothing to

do with this! Would you have sacrificed me if she hadn't come?"

"No."

"Then why her? Why anyone?"

"Because what we are asking for, what we are doing here, goes against life itself. Magic comes with a cost. And this type wants blood."

"So, you're just going to murder her?" Mystic snapped. Tears pricked behind her eyes, threatening to spill down her cheeks. She couldn't let this happen.

"This is what your client asked for! Magic is never free."

"You're a monster," Mystic breathed, allowing the first of many tears to run down her cheeks.

"I'm no different from you. You've killed thousands of sirens all in the name of a greater cause."

"That was different!" Mystic howled.

"It was not. They were innocent and in the wrong place at the wrong time. Just as Camilla is in the wrong place at the wrong time."

"She's so young. So full of life," Mystic sobbed. "Please. Don't do this."

"My people were full of life when you cut them down!" Petar bellowed. Turning on his heel, Petar moved towards the stairs. "I'll get the wench," he sneered towards the witch. "But someone will have to take her place."

PETAR

Guilt gripped the insides of Petar's stomach as his feet clambered down the damp wooden steps. The strong smell of musk and seawater filled his nostrils as he slowed his pace. His heart hammered, thumping in time with the rise and fall of his chest. Reaching the landing, he stood motionless playing back his choices.

This was the only way. The captain closed his eyes and sucked in one calming deep breath before opening them. He scanned the ship, eyeing up every hairy, burly sailor that sat or laid in hammocks, swaying left and right. He bit at his bottom lip, resting his eyes upon the dark head of curls and sighed.

His boots fell hard, echoing through the lower deck with each step the captain took until he stopped in front of the marquess. Outstretching his palm to the lady, Petar forced a smile to his lips. Large, doe-like eyes stared at his outstretched hand for several moments before crossing her arms across her ample bosom and snorting.

"I'd rather pet a rat than take your filthy hand," she sneered.

"Yer a lot less likely to catch sick, taking me hand," Petar quipped.

"I disagree." Petar sucked in another breath, trying hard to desperately to mask his rising irritation. He felt his nostrils flare as a smirk crept across the lady's face, taunting him.

"Fine," he hissed, withdrawing his hand. He shoved it into the damp pockets of his trousers and turned as if to leave. "Follow me," he said over his shoulder and headed back for the stairs.

"Why?"

"Just do it." Refusing to turn around, Petar knew Camilla had silently obeyed as her steps echoed his own. The air around him grew solemn step after step, as if he knew death was coming for him next. Before Petar could register where he was, he stood on the deck of the ship with his blood sacrifice in tow.

Laughter greeted the captain's ears as the sea witch walked past him, casting Camilla a predatory gaze. She stopped behind him and cackled again.

"Oh, she will do indeed." Camilla's dark eyes widened and the scent of fear and piss saturated his senses as he watched the girl take one step back and the witch take one forward.

"P-please," Camilla begged, taking another step back. Tears streamed down her milky cheeks. Ursulana laughed. "Please?" A game of cat and mouse played before Petar, while muffled sobs drifted into the background like music to the horror.

Camilla's scream tore from her throat, as the sea witch lunged, sinking her nails into the girl's neck. Blood poured down Camilla's chest, staining her dress red. She gurgled and choked, her eyes widening with fear as she clawed at the sea witch's hand. Scarlet blood dripped from the witch's talon-like nails as she pulled back towards her, tearing Camilla's vocal cords from her throat. Tipping her head back, Ursulana unhinged her jaw, dropping Camilla's cords down her gullet. Camilla's body hit the deck with a gentle *thud*.

Petar stood motionless and unphased, watching as a bright light surrounded the witch, consuming her in hues of white and pink. The light around her grew brighter and brighter. Petar squinted, not wanting to remove the witch from his sight. But soon, the light became too much for his siren eyes to bear. Clamping them shut, stars floated behind his lids.

When the light and the stars dissipated, Petar opened his eyes. His blood cooled in his veins. Knots formed in his stomach as he found Camilla standing before him. He'd watch the marquess die. He'd watched just moments before, her vocal cords tear from her throat and heard her body crumple to the floor, but now she stood before him, unscathed.

"Cam?" Petar choked. Camilla's lips pulled into a grin.

"Hardly," she muttered. "I'm just that good."

"You- you shifted?" the captain sputtered. The witch was good. No one would suspect Camilla Delarose dead if she stood before them. But to have someone this dangerous in Aaron's court...

"If I'm to grant your wish, then I'll do it behind the face of your regret," Ursulana cooed, taking a step towards the captain until they stood mere inches from one another. He could smell Camilla on her breath, sweet like that of a rose. Flashing the pirate a smile, Ursulana asked, "What is it you desire?"

"Death," Mystic answered coolly next to him as she wiped the mess of tears from her face. The sea witch turned to the slayer and narrowed her eyes.

"I did not ask you, mortal," she spat. As if it were dirty. As if it were wrong. But it was wrong in a sense. Petar should have never brought Mystic into the darkest parts of the Pass. Parts that he knew were evil. Parts where magic ruled freely. Being a mortal in these parts was a death sentence.

Turning, the sea witch took another step towards the captain. Petar gulped, feeling the blood rush into his cheeks, feeling dread course through his veins. She stopped only inches from Petar. Her smirk turned into a deadly grin as she pushed her new body against Petar's. He could feel every curve of the witch's form and his body reacted in ways it shouldn't. Ursulana looked up at him with her doe-like eyes and pouted her lower lip. Petar's body responded as the witch intended, with electricity and desire. Desire he hadn't felt since spending the night with Mystic.

"Kiss me," she whispered, "and I will grant your request." Petar gulped again, his pants tenting and shook his head.

"I can't. Tisn't right. Yer me blood."

"Just because we both come from the sea, doesn't mean we're related, you silly boy. I'm about as far from Poseidon as can be."

"I-I- No," Petar said firmly, pushing the witch away from him.

"I'll do it," Mystic replied from his side. He hadn't heard the slayer approach, but there she stood at his side. She slid her fingers into his and gave them a reassuring squeeze before releasing them.

"This was my mission, which makes this my request. If a kiss is what you seek, then pucker up," Mystic replied dryly. Ursulana's eyes flashed as she cocked her head to the side, her gaze lowering to Mystic and her bump.

"Fine. You don't scare me," the witch replied, puckering her lips. Petar sucked in a breath and waited. Mystic moved quickly, pushing her lips against the witch's and pulled away. It was a peck at best, but it was better than nothing. She wiped her mouth on her arm before saying, "Now, grant my wish."

Ursulana's eyebrows shot up in surprise before dropping. Her mouth spread into a wide grin as she said, "A kiss of death is what you seek."

"No. I wished death."

"To a siren," Ursulana corrected, raising her finger towards Mystic.

"How did you know?"

"Magic," the sea witch replied, biting at her lower lip, "The moment lips graze her own, her siren voice will be mine."

Petar had heard of true love's kiss and in a realm where magic ran rampant, he should have known the answer. The only one capable of destroying Serena was his best friend.

SERENA

Serena awoke to the birds singing as the world around her buzzed to life. Stifling a yawn, she thought about her brother's words and Camilla's betrayal and cocked her head to the side, relishing as her bones cracked and popped in her neck. She'd spent the last few days playing Petar's words over and over in her mind. She couldn't believe she had a half-brother. And furthermore, that he was best friends with the crown prince! But then the other half of their conversation filtered into her mind. Camilla was betraying the prince. But Serena wasn't going down that easily. If Camilla wanted a fight, well then, she would get one. Serena had time to rest and grow stronger, confining herself to her chamber. She'd practiced moving in her new body and walking without falling. She'd kicked and punched items, she'd run the laps in her room. If Camilla wanted a fight, she'd be ready.

Sunlight filtered through the princess's open window, casting shadows along the floorboards. The curtains ruffled from a light breeze, pebbling Serena's exposed arms. She closed her eyes and sucked in a deep breath, noting the smell of roses from the garden below. Her thoughts calmed, and her body relaxed back into her mattress when a knock sounded at the princess's door.

Yellow Teeth.

Serena had begun to grow accustomed to the maiden's morning routines of knocking, then sponging her clean and doing her hair, before dressing her in fine gowns and shuffling her off to breakfast with the prince. Although not much time had passed since her arrival to Andover, Serena depended on those routines. Some familiarity to cling to.

Sitting upright, she knocked back her comforter and turned to place her feet on the ground. Her stomach grumbled and Serena wondered what would be served for breakfast. A week ago, she'd hope that it was the prince. But now, she'd grown to like the prince and his company every morning. Pushing to her feet, Serena walked towards the chamber door, each step feeling like glass digging into her soles. The pain radiated up her calves. She winced but sucked in a deep breath and powered through. Every day the pain grew less and less. And with the stretches Yellow Teeth had shown her, the pain was virtually gone by midday. Reaching the door, Serena's fingers curled around the cool metal handle and turned. Pulling back, the heavy door groaned as Yellow Teeth bustled into the room.

"'Tis about time, Princess!" Yellow Teeth grumbled. Serena fought against the laughter that bubbled up from her throat, watching as the broad woman's behind swished from side to side, nearly knocking over furniture. The wooden floors creaked against her heavy footfalls as she hustled into the washroom and drew up a pail of hot soapy water.

Closing the door, Serena walked towards the window

overlooking the gardens below. She smiled as she watched pixies flutter through the air, occasionally flying high enough to give her a wave or blow a kiss. Sleep crusted the corners of her eyes as a yawn tore through the princess's body. Deciding to wait for Yellow Teeth's call, Serena walked back over to her bed and laid down, pulling her comforter over herself. She fought against the slumber that beckoned to her. But her bed was so comfortable and warm and-

"You best not be sleepin', miss!" Yellow Teeth cawed from the next room. How she knew was a mystery to the siren, but her lips perked up as heavy footfalls echoed into the bedroom.

"Miss!" Yellow Teeth hissed, storming over to Serena. "I have strict orders from the prince to get ya ready for breakfast. Come on now, let's get to it."

"Why does he want to see me?" she groaned.

"'Tis not my place to ask questions, miss. Up and at 'em!"

"I don't want to go."

"Not my place to disregard orders, miss." Yellow Teeth's heavy footfalls clambered across the floor, stopping at the edge of Serena's bed. Flooded by a cold chill, Serena felt her pull of magic from her body, a shiver racking her.

"Up!" the chambermaid hissed. Gritting her teeth, the princess sat up, hoisting her arms above her head. Yellow Teeth's nimble fingers quickly undid the night clothes the siren wore and tossed them in a heap to the ground.

"The prince is awful!" Serena grumbled as Yellow Teeth squeezed the sponge overtop of the pail. A lie. She really did care for the prince's company. But at that moment, she cared for sleep more. "Do I really have to eat breakfast with him or can I just eat him for breakfast?"

"*Miss!*" Yellow Teeth roared, fanning offense. The siren's smile grew to a grin as she imagined tearing prince Andover limb from limb. How musical his screams would be to her ears; how musical any man's screams were to her ears. As Serena lost herself into thoughts of death and murder, Yellow Teeth worked in silence, sponging her clean.

Her body glowed and burned as the water washed over her limbs, but the more she endured it, the less painful the small transformations were. Green scales broke through her flesh and the first day Yellow Teeth had sponged her clean, the pair watched with wide eyes as Serena's skin knit back together. But now, neither paid any mind to it. Both remained silent for some time before Yellow Teeth placed the sponge back into the pail and clunked back into the washroom to retrieve a towel to dry the princess with.

"But in all seriousness," Serena began, "do you know why the prince is calling upon me? It's been nearly four days since the ball, and he hasn't said a word to me. Hell, we eat breakfast in silence!"

"Not sure, miss. But I think he may fancy you a bit." Serena's eyes widened and her pulse quickened. Fancied her? *Her?*

"But-" she began before Yellow Teeth stopped and stared her straight in the eyes.

"You have to try, miss. The fate of both our kingdoms relies on you two playing nice." Serena groaned again.

Don't remind me.

"Up!" Yellow Teeth barked, pulling the princess from her spot on the bed. "Come now, stand up and we'll get ya clothed and fed."

"Must you always be so naggy?" Serena gritted out between clenched teeth. She's had just about enough of the chambermaid's bossiness for one day. Yellow Teeth rolled her eyes, turning away from the princess. She disappeared behind the partition that separated Serena's closet from the rest of her room and reemerged with six gowns draped over her arm. None were particularly fancy, though they were made of Andoverian silk. Serena found them to be nothing extraordinary other than ranging in a variety of colors.

"'Tis a bit chilly out," Yellow Teeth muttered under her breath, fumbling with gown after gown. When all were laid out on the bed, Yellow Teeth stepped back and examined them. She scratched at her bulbous chin and narrowed her gaze. After what seemed like an eternity, the chambermaid stepped forward and held up a long-sleeved pale blue gown with a black bodice. "What ye think of this one, miss?" she asked.

"It'll do," Serena replied, not caring how she looked. The mid-morning breeze bit at her skin, sending shivers through her body. She could wear a potato sack for all she cared. Anything to keep the chill away.

Yellow Teeth worked at untying the bodice and billowed the skirts on the floor, allowing the princess to step into the gown. She pulled the gown up around Serena's chilled flesh and her nimble fingers got to work tying the corset bodice around the princess's slight frame. Yellow Teeth clasped her hands to her mouth and smiled upon finishing the last knot.

"Oh my, miss. You look like a dream! We'll leave your hair down today. But you must see yourself. Go on now, take a look in the mirror!" she squeaked, wrapping her thick sausage fingers around Serena's small wrist, pulling her forward towards the mirror.

Serena took in the sight. Her hair fell in red waves past her shoulders, cupping her covered breasts. The sleeves of the dress swelled out around her arms coming to a narrow close at her pale wrists. The skirts of the dress fanned around her. As Serena stood gazing at herself in the glass, she realized how much she did look like a dream. Like a red-headed version of her deceased sister.

Ophelia.

"Now let's get some food into your belly before you do eat our prince and bring a war down on Andover," Yellow Teeth cooed, tearing the princess's gaze away from herself and her dead sister.

"Let's," Serena replied quietly, moving with grace towards her door. With one pull, the door to her chamber was open and silently, Serena made her way out into the corridor, with Yellow Teeth in tow.

THE DINING HALL WAS NEARLY EMPTY AS SERENA approached the large open doors. Each door was swathed in gold that shimmered in the chandelier lighting. The hall was bathed in hues of gold and aqua. Large golden beams ran along the cathedral-like ceiling as a large table sat in the middle of the room, littered with every food Serena could think of. Butter tarts with blueberry jam, platters of sugared plums and oranges, charred meats and plates of eggs. Serena's eyes widened; her mouth filling with saliva. Her stomach grumbled as Serena spotted the prince sitting at the end of the table, sipping on a hot cup of tea. He blew at the steam rising from the cup, pausing when his eyes met the princess's.

"Good morning, Princess."

"Is it?" Serena grumbled, plopping down into a seat across from him. The prince's lips curled into a thin smile as he took his seat.

"It is, now." Serena rolled her eyes at the silky tone of

his voice. He wanted to charm the bejabbers out of her and it wasn't going to work. She flicked her tongue over her tooth, light enough to feel it's prick, but not draw blood, and took a deep breath. It was going to be another long, silent breakfast. Grabbing for the sugared tarts and smoked meat, Serena shoveled morsel after morsel into her mouth like a savage. She couldn't remember what the food tasted like, just that her hunger pangs were subsiding.

"Why are you such an arse?" Serena snapped, swallowing her mouth full of food, breaking the silence. "You live in the most beautiful place, surrounded by magic and – you're just horrible!" Aaron froze with a piece of meat on his fork and lowered it. His steely stare met her own, cool and collected. His jaw set and his face hardened.

"Great. I'm so glad you got that off your chest. I can't wait to hear how horrible you think I am all afternoon."

"See! Now that's what I'm talking about!" Serena retorted.

"Gods, Serena! Can't you just stop? Can't we just have one meal where you don't hate me and I don't fantasize about all the things I want to do to you?"

"Come again?" she sputtered, lowering her gaze from his scrutiny to her tart-covered hands. Her heart quickened in her chest for reasons she couldn't quite understand.

"Just… never mind," Aaron sighed and returned his attention back on his food. Silence hung heavy between the pair, waiting for someone to break it. But Serena didn't know what to say. No one had ever spoken to her that way. Had ever put her in her place, well, besides Aramis. And now, the prince was saying things she couldn't quite understand. Things she wasn't sure she was ready to understand and accept. Grabbing for a cloth napkin, Serena worked at removing the tart filling from her nails and pouted as she replied, "Fine."

Breakfast hadn't gone quite as Serena had planned. She'd wanted to get under the prince's skin and fester her words there like an infected wound, but somehow, he had managed to get into her head and corrupt her thoughts. Every notion of the prince caused her pulse to quicken and blood to rush into her cheeks. He had a hold on her, and she'd be damned if he knew it.

Breakfast had finished in silence and Serena had been left to her own devices until the prince called for her again. But that was hours ago. Now, they sat on a small boat in the middle of a pond on the outskirts of the castle, surrounded with water lilies and trees that curtained the shore. She wasn't sure why Aaron had brought her here, to a place so remote that no one would hear them if something happened. She should have been suspicious, should have stolen a weapon away under her skirts. But after the prince's words at breakfast, she wasn't sure if she could go through with her mission.

"Can't we just have one meal where you don't hate me and I don't fantasize about all the things I want to do to you?" What did that even mean?

As the pair sat alone on the water, Serena observed Aaron. She watched the muscles in his chest tense and release with every push and pull of the oars. She watched as his skin slickened with droplets of sweat and memorized the way that his white linen shirt clung to his torso. The spot between her thighs tingled the longer she watched him. *"Can't we just have one meal where you don't hate me?"* His words rang through her mind. She didn't hate him. Right? *"…and I don't fantasize about all the things I want to do to you?"* Sucking in a deep breath, Serena let out a sigh. She was so confused. What did he mean? What did this all mean? And why did she feel like this?

"Why are you staring at me?" Aaron asked, his voice piercing through the silence. "Do I have something on my face?" His brows creased and his gaze narrowed on Serena. The princess gulped and looked away.

"No, sorry," was all she managed to get out. Her eyes studied his face, noting the sharp curve of his jaw. The way he bit at his lower lip as he rowed the oars. The way he was looking at her with a predatory glint in his eye. Serena watched as Aaron lowered the oars; his muscles flexed in his arms.

"I thought this would be a good place for us to get to know one another," he said and leaned back on his arms. "So, tell me, what do you do for fun?" That's what he wanted to know? What she did for fun? She wanted to know the damn meaning of his cryptic words.

"I drown men, devour them and then lie in the sun," Serena replied, pretending to fan herself. Aaron smiled and slowly shook his head as a small laugh escaped his lips.

"Well aren't you terse." Warmth flowed through Serena as she met the prince's blue eyes. "How many Andoverian men have you killed in your lifetime?"

"I don't know. I don't discriminate when it comes to kills. I've killed Alcoverans, Andoverian and some from lands far away from here."

"Well now that your killing spree is over, per the treaty, what would you say is your second hobby?"

"I sing." It was as if her words lit a fire within the prince. His eyes glittered with excitement as he sat up straight and clasped Serena's hands within his own.

"Will you sing for me?" he asked, leaning forward. The boat wobbled on the serene water as Aaron awaited her answer.

"Do you have a death wish?" The prince's brows furrowed causing two small ditches to form above the bridge of his nose. His nose crinkled as he digested her words.

"What do you mean?" he asked.

"I sing to trap men like you into watery graves," Serena replied matter-of-factly.

"I see," Aaron said, scratching at his dark locks. "Well, perhaps someday you'll find the courage to sing for me without eating me."

"Perhaps."

Perhaps, indeed. But today was not that day. Aaron curled his fingers into a fist and released a cough, clearing his throat before saying, "I thought we would spend the day out here getting to know one another."

"You said that already. But, why should we bother? You hate me and I hate you. So, what is the point of all of this? If anything, you're just torturing me." The prince's eyes widened as Serena's words hit home. Aaron diverted his gaze as a look of hurt spread over his features.

"I don't hate you. Far from it actually."

"Then why didn't you call upon me after the ball?" Serena spat, crossing her arms. Before she could even process her words, Aaron's eyes met her.

"I-is that what you're mad about?"

"No. Yes. I don't know. Maybe." Aaron's chiseled jaw set, the veins in his temple flaring to life as he cocked his head to the side and licked his lips.

"I didn't call upon you because you nearly died in my garden!"

"Wait, you knew about that?"

"Of course, I knew! I couldn't bear to see you uncon-scious! You undo me, Serena. There's something about you that drives me crazy. You enchant me and it kills me to not be with you. I know this isn't the life you chose and it's not what I wanted either. But seeing you here, seeing you persevere…" Aaron trailed off, swallowing as his eyes flashed back to hers. "I need you. And I think you need me too. And seeing you there in that bed, it broke me."

Serena's lungs burned as she let out her breath. Her eyes pooled with tears she'd been fighting back. But it was no use. They spilled from overtop of her eyes and trailed down her cheeks. Aaron leaned forward and reached out towards her. His finger skimmed along her cheek, catching her tears.

"Because if I lost you, I'd lose everything," he whispered and pushed his lips into Serena's.

He was fire to her ice, melting Serena's insides as she gripped the prince's face. His lips grazed against her own, sucking the breath from Serena's lungs. His lips moved with hers with an abrupt hunger.

She wanted this.

She needed this.

Needed *him*.

It was as if he was telling her everything without speaking. The flower between Serena's legs ached to be touched, ached to blossom, driving her over the edge. She slid her tongue along the prince's lower lips, beckoning him to allow her in. Shifting, Aaron cupped both sides of the siren's face, deepening their kiss before abruptly pulling away. Serena's eyes opened as her lungs begged for air. Aaron's own chest heaved, and blood rushed into his cheeks and pants.

Embarrassed, he stood and turned away from her, grabbing for an oar. Serena grinned. She'd made him feel something. Hell, he'd confessed his feelings for her! Of course, she made him feel something! Pushing his frustrations through the water, Aaron steered the boat towards a clearing in the trees. Serena watched as the curtain of trees around them opened up. She opened her mouth, calling to her siren voice. But, when nothing came to her, the siren clutched at her throat.

Something was terribly wrong.

AARON

aron's mind whirled with life as he pushed the boat towards the shore. He hadn't anticipated kissing the siren, but something within him changed. He wanted to be with her. The one person who would feel the same way he did. Neither chose this path, yet here they were. He'd spent so long hating her people for the bloodshed they caused in his realm, but it never affected him. He hadn't lost anyone close to him, but Serena had. Her sister, her father and now her home. The walls he'd built around his heart crumbled.

He was stupid.

So *stupid*.

Why did he kiss her? Was it an impulse? Perhaps. But there had been a spark and he'd felt it on his lips. His deadly attraction was to the one girl he knew could heal him. And maybe, he could heal her too.

Aaron's fingers ached as he squeezed the oar in his hand, feeling as though they would seize up on him in a moment's notice, growing from pink to red to white. It was strange, really, how he could like the creature behind him.

She was fierce and deadly but also had a sweetness about her. His lips perked into a weak smile as he thought about Serena's eyes taking in the drooping willow trees around them or the pixies that skittered in and out of the branches. Everything about this world, *his* world, was new and exciting to her. And she was new and exciting to *him*.

Out in the clearing, the midday sun hung high in the cloudless blue sky. The cool air around them whipped up, chilling the sweat on the prince's brow. Water lilies floated in the pond around them, filling Aaron's nose with their tangy aroma. Aaron's muscles relaxed, lowering the oar slightly as he closed his eyes. His mother had worn something similar in his youth, long before her untimely death. The brief scent sent a river of memories, flooding through the prince's mind. He remembered the glitter of his mother's cerulean eyes and her white-blonde locks. Her determination to prove to the kingdom that, she, too, could be a queen. Serena was a lot like her. Determined and strong and a lot smarter than he was.

Serena hadn't said anything after their kiss, and Aaron didn't know if it was shock or anger that stripped the words from her tongue as the silence loomed around them. Sucking in a deep breath, Aaron opened his eyes and raked his fingers through his dark, silky tresses before he turned to face the siren. Serena's eyes were wide, stricken with fear as she clasped at her throat. Her fingers froze, curling midair as their eyes met.

"I'm sorry," Aaron murmured, scratching at his scalp. He was sorry. Sorry, he loved her. Sorry, he'd brought her here. There were so many things he should have apologized for. Regret coursed through his veins and gnawed at the prince's insides.

Serena cocked her head to the right, looking much like a puppy hearing a new sound. Her red hair fell to her side in waves and at that moment, Aaron's heart pumped a little faster. His lips lifted, widening into a wolfish grin before he could stop himself.

Yup. He was dumb and done and he knew it… but he didn't care.

"Well, this is not how this trip was supposed to go," he began. "I'm no smoother than a ship's barnacle, but for the love of Zeus the Almighty, please say something, Anything?" Pushing his thumbs into his eyes, the prince winced. His ears rang and his heart hammered against his ribcage, threatening to break free. His lungs burned, begging for air and that's when Aaron realized he had been holding his breath, waiting for a response. But when none came, he rubbed his face some more and sat down on the narrow seat behind him.

"Please, say something," he groaned. "Anything." Serena's eyes narrowed as she opened her mouth and pointed before dropping her hands into her lap.

"Huh?" Aaron asked, cocking a brow. Serena rolled her eyes and pointed at her mouth again. Huffing a breath, Serena's face scrunched as though she was mustering up her song to enchant him before a watery grave.

Aaron waited to hear her sing just like she had on the docks when they'd arrived in Andover. He waited for her voice to consume him, ruin him. Silence devoured the prince's aching thoughts, feeding his soul with a crushing defeat. Aaron watched Serena. Watched the tears gather in her eyes and slip down her milky cheeks. He watched as she again tried to sing but fell short. A chill ran down the prince's spine as he put two and two together.

She couldn't sing.

Because for whatever reason her voice was no more. Aaron knew that there was only one thing strong enough to steal a siren's voice.

Dark magic.

Where there was darkness, there would be a wielder.

"I will find the scum that stole your voice," he vowed quietly, reaching forward in the boat. His fingers brushed against the siren's cool boney ones and gave them a reassuring squeeze. "And when I do. They will pay."

ANGER FLARED THROUGH AARON'S VEINS AS HE STORMED through the castle halls. Someone had the audacity to taint his *bride* with darkness. To steal her voice. To threaten the crown prince and his throne. The prince's vision clouded around the edges, and Aaron knew that soon his blood would boil hot with pure rage. His vision would become a veil of black and then, well, anything could happen. Power surged through his body, a white light, his mother had once called it, but something never to be tempted. If he allowed his anger to reach its peak, his own magic would be released. The very magic that flowed through his veins and bound him to the throne. If his power was released, another life would be lost. Bile lurched up the prince's throat as he rounded the corner. He couldn't let his power kill again. His mother had been a horrible *accident* and gods did he wish he could take it back. Hot tears pricked at the corners of Aaron's eyes as he approached a staircase, laden with white marble and gold.

"You're just another mistake," his father's voice echoed through his memories. "Your mother would still be here if it wasn't for you."

He was a burden.

A monster.

Murderer.

Ragged breaths shuddered through the prince's body, his chest tightened as the tears that Aaron so desperately fought against, spilled over his lashes. Pain, so much pain, escaping the shell of the man he'd hidden away for too long.

"Pull yourself together, boy," his father's voice echoed. *"We still have a kingdom to rule and a war to end."* Aaron sniffled and wiped the tears from his cheeks. He needed to pull himself together and focus on Serena. She was what mattered now. She was his future.

Tapestries coated the stone walls as Aaron began his ascent, taking stair after stair towards his father's study. Shimmers of gold danced in the prince's vision as the flames of sconces danced across the decadent floors and railings. Each step was a stab against his ego. He wasn't strong enough to protect his mother... or *Serena*. He wasn't intimidating enough to ward off an attack, and why would he be? Every decision was made for him. He was a pawn in his father's realm. A puppet for his father to manipulate.

Flicking his tongue against his canines, Aaron glowered and moved faster. He would find the bastard responsible and then he would teach them a lesson. Cursing his bride was a threat against the throne and his reign, and he would be damned if he allowed such actions to be swept under the rug. Aaron's heart thrummed faster with each step he took, and as his mind whirled, he found himself standing in front of his father's study. He would prove himself worthy. He would fix this mess and rule the kingdom with a siren bride at his side.

The large oak door stood ajar as whispered voices trailed into the hall. Silently, the prince approached, sidling up to the wall and listened.

"The boy is nearly a means to an end," his father said. Aaron moved closer, peering inside. He spotted his father sitting at a round table with his seneschal and advisors. "With Adrella on our side, we can begin our conquest into other kingdoms."

"And what of the girl?" a female voice quipped.

"Mitera has the girl hidden away in a tower of stone, deep inside the Forest of Broken Souls. We can use her, use Ira's life-giving light, to conquer Bellamy's lands."

"And what of Aaron?"

"What of him?" King Marlow grumbled.

"Does he know about her?" his seneschal asked. Aaron peered in further, seeing the seneschal for the first time. His father's advisors stayed hidden away from him. From the kingdom, whether for their safety or some other reason, Aaron didn't know.

"Aaron knows what I want him to know. He is heir to the gold throne, and even that was a stretch. The boy is lucky enough that Andover has rules. But I do not need him. Azalea is the key."

Anger roiled deep within Aaron, sending electric shocks through his veins. His magic calling to him, begging him to be set free. Aaron stood for a moment, his father's words ringing through his head, and sucked in a deep breath before doing the very thing he knew could end his reign before it began.

Pushing aside the door, he strode in. The king's seneschal jumped, drawing a sword fastened at her hip. He hadn't seen it through the small crack in the door, but that didn't matter now. His father turned his steely expression on him.

"What are you doing here, boy?" he gritted out between clenched teeth.

"I want to know the truth. You've been lying to me my entire life. It ends now." King Marlow cocked a brow, his lips pulling into a smirk before releasing the king's haughty laughter.

"You do not know what you're talking about. Go, before things get hard for you." Hard for him? *Hard for him?* Aaron's vision blurred along the edges, tunneling before going completely black. He'd fought against his magic for so long, but now, it was being set free. His nerves felt alive with electricity, pouring into his fingertips. Then there was a scream.

A woman's scream. Just like there had been that dreadful night. The floor beneath Aaron began to shake, the castle rumbling before a deafening crack erupted through the air. Rubble fell from the ceiling, coating Aaron in a shower of dust.

Another scream, this time male. Perhaps it was his father? Or a guard. Aaron couldn't tell as his body gave in to the magic, allowing it to flow freely from him. He could smell something burning, filtering into his nostrils.

"Aaron!" his father shouted before another crack of lightning hit. "Stop! I'll tell you everything!"

Lightning crashed near him, splintering wood, crackling flames to life.

"Please, boy!" his father begged. "Do not be a king slayer. Please, Aaron." Aaron felt his body growing heavy, his magic slowly ebbing back to the fiery depths where it had laid dormant for so long. Slowly, his vision returned and before he knew it, he was falling. Arms grasped Aaron around the waist, lowering him into the little bit of chair that had been spared. His eyes drooped, but he was finally going to hear some answers.

Azalea.

Who was she?

And did she hold the key to Serena's voice?

Sucking in a deep breath, Aaron made a silent vow before the exhaustion took hold. He would find the girl in the stone tower and with it, find Serena's voice.

ARAMIS

Sitting upon her crystal throne, Aramis thrummed her fingers against the cool armrest and thought of her younger sister. It had been nearly two weeks since Aramis had delivered her sister on a silver platter to the land king. Her intentions had been clear: Kill the crown and take the land for Adrella. She had faith that Serena would get the job done. There was no doubt that Marlow and his son would die in a bloodbath, and the land would suffer under Serena's rule. But two weeks was surely too long. She should have heard news by now. Something, anything about the treaty being broken. But there was nothing. Court was quiet and no gossip roamed the crystal halls. She'd shown no mercy towards Serena during her final days in Adrella, and if she knew better, Serena would channel her tortured feelings and relinquish them onto the king. So why hadn't anything happened?

Sucking in a deep breath, the queen let out an annoyed sigh. Her tail flicked from left to right. A twitch she'd had ever since she was young and ground her teeth. Pinching the bridge of her nose between her forefinger and thumb, Aramis caught an image of Shay approaching silently from her right. Aramis adjusted herself back into her regal pose and turned to face her seneschal. Aramis raked her gaze up and down Shay, licking her lips and imagining the delectable noises she could summon from her right hand. Shay may have the most suitors in her kingdom, but she also had the queen's fancy. Lowering herself into the seat next to the queen, Shay said nothing.

"Shay," Aramis said coolly, turning to face her friend. "What news have you got?"

"The sprites refuse to speak, Your Majesty."

"Did you threaten our cousins for answers?"

"No, my lady," Shay replied, her voice barely audible. Leaning forward, Aramis outstretched her right hand and cupped Shay's cocoa cheeks, grazing her nails along her cool flesh.

"Puppet," she cooed. "Threaten their demise and get my answers, or the next time you take a seat beside me, it will be your last," she said, moving her hand from Shay's cheek to her hair. Her fingers twisted between her friend's silken locks, knotting at the base of Shay's skull. Pulling her advisor until the two sat nose to nose, Aramis whispered, "Understood?" before grazing Shay's lips with her own. Shay swallowed hard and nodded silently.

Aramis smiled, "Go, puppet. Get my answers." Shay bustled up from her seat and swam quickly away from the queen, refusing to look back. Alone once more, Aramis slouched, returning her fingers to their agitated thrum on her armrest. She flicked her tongue over her teeth and straightened abruptly. If she wanted things done right, then she needed to take matters into her own hands. She would make an unexpected visit to the land and watch her sister's bloodbath unfold before her, or she would do it herself.

To the Underworld with the Treaty, she thought before pushing from her throne.

DARKNESS SHROUDED ARAMIS AS SHE BREACHED THE surface. She'd swum an entire day and night to get to the cursed land. Blue light surrounded the queen as she swam towards the shoreline, her ascension beginning. Rowboats and ships lined the port docks without a soul in sight as she drew closer. She knew what was next and sucked in a deep breath, holding out for the moment her tail tore into two. She pushed her tail and arms as quickly as they would go towards the docks, clinging onto the sodden wood of the pier, hoisting herself up.

Purple blood seeped into the water and tears ran down the queen's face. She'd lied to Serena. The transformation never got better, and she had not grown used to the pain but instead dealt with it. She'd wanted to scream, to curse the Fates and Poseidon and anything that would listen to her insults, but kept her lips shut and her thoughts to herself.

As the seconds passed into minutes, the pain in Aramis grew with the light around her. The queen opened her mouth to scream and then everything ceased. The pain, the light, everything. There she stood, Queen of Adrella, naked and soaked to the bone on a land where she was not welcome. Tears brimmed her eyes as she crossed her arms to shield her bare breasts from the cold that bit at her skin, and took one heavy step after another out of the waters, she called *home*.

Cold.

Naked.
Alone.
Vulnerable.
Aramis stood onshore without a soul in the world to greet her and wept.

PETAR

*P*etar's stomach coiled in on himself as he clung to the helm. Nausea clawed at his throat as he fought down the singing bile that crept up. Doubling over, Petar emptied the remainder of his stomach contents onto the ship's deck as they traveled back towards Andover. He'd succeeded in destroying Camilla and saving his sister, but a bigger threat now sailed to shore with him and that was not something he could handle.

Ursulana. Sweat peppered the captain's brow, trailing down into his eyes. Using the sleeve of his shirt, Petar wiped the beads away. He'd never been one for seasickness, and often berated his crew for such weakness, but here and now, he felt like death. His body hated him. Like a punch to the gut, Petar curled over, clutching at his stomach before spewing another load onto the floorboards.

How could he bring the witch back to Andover? How could Mystic have sealed their fates? Fear gripped the captain as he thought about their baby. What type of danger had he brought unto them? Andover would never be safe again. It would be a tale told in horror. About a beast none could slay, and a land cursed. They couldn't raise their child there. Not now.

Sucking in a shallow breath, Petar steadied himself and pushed upright, wiping bile from his lips. He had to fix this and warn Aaron. He couldn't sit by and let his home fall. Looking out into the deck below, Petar glimpsed Mystic, who locked eyes with him, flashing a toothy grin. Petar's heart beat faster in his chest as his eyes glanced to her growing midsection.

She was growing larger by the day. Although she hadn't been with child long, her pregnancy would be over in just a few short weeks. Magic flowed through the slayer's veins, through his child. As if sensing his gaze, Mystic moved her hand over her growing belly and smiled weakly before waving him over again. With a defeated sigh, Petar called out to his first mate, a lad by the name of Max, and instructed him to steer the helm. Short in stature, Max stood no taller than the captain's shoulder. He was lanky with dark hair that trailed down to his shoulders and flew around his head in a halo as the ocean's breeze took hold of it. Max was the brother Petar never had, finding him slumming in the ports of Swallow Hallow, an island just south of Alcovera on the Adrellan seas at the ripe age of ten. Petar remembered that day like it was yesterday and remembered the gleam in Max's hazel eyes when he'd offered him a job and a home upon the *Camilla Delarose*. Max had taken to sailing quickly and now, no more than seventeen years old, he knew his way around a ship like it was nobody's business.

"Aye, aye, Captain!" Max replied, saluting Petar. Unfurling his fingers from the wheel, Petar set out towards Mystic. She was his everything. Step by step he took until he was on the lower deck and by Mystic's side. His fingers wrapped around her own as he moved behind Mystic's small frame and held her close. Petar leaned in, placing his cheek against Mystic's own chestnut complexion and inhaled before pressing his lips to her ear.

"I love you," he whispered. "Will you marry me?" He could feel the slayer's body grow rigid before releasing his fingers. She turned to face him; her eyes wide with surprise.

"Why now?" she asked.

"What?"

"Why now?" she repeated. "You weren't ready to settle down back in port, so why now and why me?"

"Isn't me love enough fer ye?" Petar choked out.

"I wish it were. I wish it were that simple, but no, it's not enough."

"I have me own reasons. All of which stem from me love fer ye."

"A baby is not enough to stay with me. You love me now, but what about ten years from now? Will you love me then? Will you really be happy staying in a small port cottage with a wife and child to tend to? I love you too much to chain you. I love you too much to have you resent me."

"Me heart belongs to ye, Mystic Brooksborough, and to the wee babe that ye carry. Me soul will always belong to the sea, but me heart no longer does. Please," he nearly begged. Pain ripped through the captain. His heart was shattering. Moments ago, they were in bliss. And now she wanted to leave him? What had he done wrong? He was willing to give up everything to be with her and their child. His life was falling apart before his eyes and he could do nothing. The slayer turned and gripped the side of the ship, looking out into the sunrise.

"I'm sorry," she whispered, shadowing her face from view.

Petar's vision clouded as his stomach twisted, knotting in on itself. Darkness muddled the corners of his eyes and his breathing halted. His life was over. Tears rolled silently down the pirate's cheek, and Petar knew he should wipe them away, hide them from his crew, but he had no fight left in him. Closing his eyes, he pinched at the bridge of his nose and brow and steadied his racing thoughts. If the slayer didn't want him, then he would have to fix this. Have to prove himself to her. And how could he do that while unraveling at the seams?

"Fine," he snapped. "Then get out of my sight."

"Excuse me?" Mystic whirled, placing a hand on her hip, her fingers thrumming on the bulge of her belly.

"Get. Out. Of. My. Sight," he growled, flashing the points of his serrated teeth. Taking a step forward, Petar puffed out his chest and loomed over the slayer. "Leave before I do something, we both won't forget," he gritted out between clenched teeth. But Mystic didn't back down. Placing her other hand on the hilt of Siren Blade she took a step forward. Petar was a good two feet taller than his counterpart.

"You dare to threaten me? Just because I'm pregnant doesn't mean I can't kick your arse!" she hissed. "I'm not afraid of you and if you come any closer, I will gut you like a fish." Like a stick poking at a sleeping bear, Petar's vicious instincts kicked in. His nails grew into pointed daggers and the beast within him laughed.

"Funny. Because the babe growing within you shares me fish blood and magic. You want to gut me? Then cut the *siren* child from your belly!" Mystic's eyes widened, her jaw slacked before dropping open, as her gaze dropped to her growing belly. Silently, she shook her head.

"No," she whispered. "That's impossible."

"It's not."

"But h-how?" she asked, her voice breaking as her eyes filled with tears. Petar felt the corners of his mouth perk. He had her now. If she didn't love him enough to marry him, then she could hate him and *herself*.

"Because I'm a siren, you stupid wench!" Sinking to her knees, Mystic released a blood-curdling howl. Sobs wracked her body, shaking her small frame violently.

"You're a monster," she shrieked.

"Perhaps," was all Petar replied before ordering two crew members to pick up the grief-stricken slayer and haul her away. Her cries echoed off into the distance, but Petar didn't care. She'd shattered him and in turn, he'd destroyed her. He returned focus to the water ahead and turned on his heel, heading up the steps to the upper deck where Max stood steering the helm. He gave the boy a curt nod before taking his place. Petar peered into the horizon and past that, Andover's port.

DUSK DESCENDED UPON ANDOVER HOURS AFTER PETAR's ship docked. He'd spent most of his evening smoking in Andover's taverns and flirting with drunken barmaids. His heart hurt and his ego had taken a blow. Swigging back a pint of honey ale, Petar pushed from his stool onto wobbly legs. He sucked in a breath before shoving his hand into the tan trench coat he'd bought upon entering port and fished out three gold coins with Aaron's face on them. It was more than enough to pay for his time spent in the establishment. One wobbly step after another, the pirate pushed through the tavern's russet double doors into the brisk night.

The groan of fiddles and violins filled his ears while passersby rushed home, deserting the cobblestone roads. It was a moment of clarity for the young captain. He was alone, or well, nearly.

Heel to toe, Petar placed his feet as he walked. He couldn't slip and fall if he was watching his feet, right?

Moonlight lit the path from the tavern and Petar's sober brain knew that he should just take the cobblestone path straight to the castle, but his intoxicated brain thought otherwise. The crash of waves called to his soul like a song to soothe a crying baby. He obeyed and strayed from his path. His heels scuffed again dirt and grass lumps as his legs begged for him to stop and relax, but Petar pushed onward until he was at the water's edge. Mist and salt showered the captain as his eyes locked onto a darkened figure, emerging from the trees down the way.

She was naked and beautiful, but something was off. Had the captain been in his right state of mind, he would have been able to place it. But right then, all he wanted was to swoop in and be the lass's knight in shining armor.

Pulling the tan trench jacket from his biceps, Petar draped it over his arm before stumbling towards the figure.

"Meeeeee laddddy," Petar slurred, dipping his head and hat low into a bow. "A prettay 'ittle thing like yourself, shouldn't be out in these parts without clothes." The figure remained silent. Huffing a breath, the captain threw the jacket towards her, watching as the coat hit the sand.

"Thank you," he heard whispered between sobs before the figure bent to retrieve the article. Petar smiled and turned away, pushing his way back up the hill he came from. He wobbled for a moment, grasping at the air before finding his footing on the cobble path that would take him to the castle.

It wasn't long before Petar had reached the castle. Ebony painted the sky and sconces danced to life with flames in the arched entrance of the castle. Two guards, clad in golden armor, stood outside the golden gate, blocking Petar's path.

"Ge' ot er me way!" Petar slurred, fishing in his trouser pocket for his smokes. His fingers curled around the small cigarette and pulled it free from his pocket. Lifting his fingers to his lips, Petar lit his smoke to life and sucked in a drag. A familiar ease clouded his body, releasing the tension built from the day. Petar relished the buzz and the mind-numbing ecstasy that followed.

"State your business," the guard on the left announced, wrinkling his nose in disgust as Petar took another long drag. Exhaling, Petar replied, "Aaron."

"The prince is not taking visitors," the guard on the right remarked.

"Piss off, sodskull. I live 'ere too. Now, open the durs." The pair of guards turned, giving one another a look of defeat and shrugged.

"Sorry, mate, can't let you in past dusk. King's orders. Find somewhere else to sleep for the night."

"I'll kill ye come morn," Petar muttered, sidling up to the cold stone of the castle. He pressed back into the rock and sat, curling his arms around his bent knees and shut his eyes. "And if any of ye thinks to steal me smokes, I'll kill ye *before* morn."

AARON

*A*aron rolled his eyes, gnashing his teeth together, silently seething. His best friend had been denied entry into the castle, the very man that Aaron indeed wanted to see. Power surged through the prince's veins as his messenger, a young male no older than the age of sixteen or so, continued to spew news at him in his chambers. His golden hair curled at the ends and his blue eyes cast down towards the wooden floor. The boy reminded Aaron of Petar during his youth and something within the prince softened.

"Get him out of the cold," he said softly, masking his irritation enough to ease the kid, "and bring him here. Then bring me the idiots who denied his entry."

"Yes, Your Royal Highness," the messenger murmured scurrying out of Aaron's decadent chambers. He needed to get himself under control, needed to find Serena's voice and destroy the dark magic before the wielder did much worse. Aaron walked to the large chamber window carved into the castle itself and watched the gardens below. He loved watching the nymphs and pixies play, and the array of bright colors that grew with every flower, leaf, and bush. He'd been surrounded by magic his entire life, wielded it inside himself and witnessed its beauty and destruction. Darkness was creeping into his lands. Something that raised every hair on his body. Something he was unsure he could fight off alone.

A knock on the door startled the prince, tearing him from his thoughts as he moved to answer his caller. *It better be Petar*, he thought. They had so much to catch up on. Stopping midway to the door, something caught the prince's attention, freezing him in place.

"Come in!" he bellowed, his voice echoing off the stone walls. Tink, laden in a harvest leaf dress, swarmed around his room, looking a bit disoriented. Aaron's brows furrowed as his chamber door creaked open. He'd never seen the pixie disoriented, tainted by something powerful, she fell from the air. Racing towards her, Aaron outstretched his hand, catching the pixie midair.

"Oh Tink," he whispered. Footsteps clattered against his floor as Petar moved swiftly inside, closing the door behind him.

"Why the bloody barnacle was I locked from the castle, Aaron?" he hissed, his eyes flicking to Aaron's palm. The prince cupped Tink's small frame.

"Was not my intention and the guards responsible will be punished, but that's not why I called you here." Aaron's face grew dim. Tink's body trembled and her wings skittered to a stop, dropping low to her back. "Dark magic has taken hold in Andover."

"What do ye mean?" Petar asked, his face scrunching in pain as he held out his hand to Aaron, scooping Tink into his own palms. Tink looked up at the captain, shuddering again before dropping to a knee.

"What's one thing that is strong enough to take away a siren's voice and poison our lands?" Aaron asked.

"Oh Tink," Petar whispered, "I'm so sorry," he said, kissing the pixie gently on her head. Tears ran down the captain's cheeks as he wiped them away with his shirt sleeve.

"Petar, did you hear me?"

"Why did ye phrase it like that?" Petar asked, raising his eyes from Tink.

"Something happened. Serena, she's lost her voice. She can't talk, can't sing and I think that dark magic has cursed her and soon it will curse our lands. But there's a cure. My father said there was a girl that held magical powers, locked in a tower deep in the forests. She is the key to everything. He said it himself."

"No," Petar pinched the bridge of his nose. "No, no! You sodskull, did ye kiss the girl?" Dipping his chin low, Aaron's heart raced as he thought about Serena's soft, supple lips against his own. Blood rushed into his cheeks and he could feel them heat. He tried desperately to hide the blush from his face, turning away from his friend.

"Ye Idiot! What have ye done?" Petar hissed.

"Huh?"

"The sea witch has cursed ye both." Cursed them both?

"The darkness... How do you know these things, Petar?" he spat out.

"Errm, because I may have summoned her to save Serena."

"You what?" Aaron bellowed, feeling the pull of his magic, deep within him, begin to bubble.

"You dunderhead! Now you're going to help me reverse the curse and you're going to tell Serena what happened."

"But—" Petar began. Aaron held out his hand, silencing the captain before an excuse could escape his parted lips. Aaron didn't want to hear it. He didn't know how his friend had saved Serena, but he did know that the witch would destroy them all.

"Go!" he snarled.

SERENA

Anger tore through Serena as she stormed through the castle halls, throwing open the door to her chamber, striding inside. Magic gripped at her throat, silencing her tongue. Silencing the only weapon she had to defend herself on land, leaving her vulnerable. *Human.* Serena paced in her chamber, racking her brain on what to do next. Surely the curse on her voice could be broken, but how? That was what she needed to find out. Curling her fingers into fists, Serena's nails burrowed into her palms, slicing the skin. Sharp pain seeped from her hand, slick with blood and dripped in small droplets onto the floor below. Someone very powerful did this to her. Aramis? Wait, no. Why would her sister do this to her? She was keeping the bloodshed between the kingdoms at bay. Unless she did it to spite her?

Serena's stomach grumbled, sending aching pain through her body. When was the last time she'd eaten? Breakfast? But there was no way she could eat now. She was *broken.* Her stomach knotted at the thought and a part of Serena wanted to feel bad for herself. Wanted to curl up into a ball on her four-poster bed and weep until there was nothing left in her body. A part of her wanted to give up and die. For a moment, Serena wondered if she did die in Andover, would she turn to foam like a normal siren or rot in a human meat suit six feet in the ground? The princess shook her head and continued to pace. Sunlight peeked through the curtains, casting slivers of gold into the room. Slivers of hope.

"Hope is for the lonely and will only get you killed." Her sister's parting words. But hope was all she had left.

"Get yourself together," a voice rang out, echoing through the chamber. Serena's pace faltered as her body tensed.

Aramis?

This was all a dream, right?

No.

She was hallucinating. Clearly, she was losing her damned mind.

Right?

The air around the princess hung heavy with magic, clinging to her skin. Every nerve within the siren felt alive and on edge. Serena's feet halted in place. Invisible fingers gripped at her throat, at the voice that was no longer there. Her vision swam with tiny specks as an outline of black appeared from the shadows. Serena blinked, rubbing at her eyes with her palms, but the figure continued to approach. Her lips parted as laughter bubbled up her throat, bursting free. Serena's body quaked, but no sound escaped her. She should have cared. She should have felt fear. But at that moment, Serena didn't mind. She was going crazy, after all.

She laughed until her ribs ached and her eyes welled with warm tears. She was going stark raving mad, because there was no way she'd lost her own voice and heard her sister's disembodied one. There was definitely no way her sister was standing before her wearing nothing but a dirtied trench coat to cover her otherwise naked body.

"Stop laughing," Aramis hissed. Tendrils of magic snaked down Serena's throat, seizing the laughter. Her body stilled, growing rigid. Serena's head pounded, her body ached, as her sister's magic took hold. This was no hallucination. Aramis was here and she was *mad*. Question after question filled Serena's mind, things she wanted to ask, but had no means to. How did she find her? How did she go through the castle in a trench coat, undetected? Why was she here?

Serena lowered her gaze to the floor, dipping her head in a respectful bow. Dread coursed through her veins as she curtsied to her sister, something she'd never done. A human custom learned during her short time in Andover.

"No greeting for your queen?" Aramis snarled. Serena gulped and snapped her head up, her attention solely on the queen. She opened her mouth to speak, to offer up a retort, but only silence greeted her elder sister. A smile played on the queen's cruel lips as she continued, "What would Ophelia think if she saw you right now?"

Serena shifted uncomfortably from foot to foot. Bringing Ophelia into this was a low blow. Sirens did not speak of their dead in such terms. Did not flaunt them so cavalierly. She watched the queen's lip curl, exposing her scored fangs. She knew her sister struck an unspeakable chord, but Serena remained silent. *Like she had a choice!* Her eyes focused on Aramis and the veins bulging in her neck and face. Anger, true, unadulterated anger, was not becoming on the queen. The lack of response from Serena was sending her into an outright rage. No one showed the throne disrespect and lived.

"Fine. Enough simple talk. Let's get down to the reason

I'm here," the queen cooed, taking another step into Serena's view. "I expected to hear from you by now, Serena. It's not like you to play with your food for so long. But with the court quiet with news, I knew something was up. Obviously, King Marlow and his brat still live. Which bears the question—when do you plan to kill the prince?"

A chill ran down Serena's spine, shuddering at the thought. She hadn't pondered her mission since arriving in Andover and despite how much she fought it, she had started to like the place. She'd fallen for the magic her new home held, amongst other things. The prince treated her fair, had welcomed her into his home, his lands and granted her all the amenities she would need to live comfortably. He'd shown her the gardens, his secret place to hide away and taught her to dance and to trust. He'd shown her compassion when no one else had and made her feel.

He made her—*human.*

Serena swallowed back the lump that formed in her throat as her emotions plummeted into her. That arrogant princeling had worked his way into her heart and made her walls come crashing down.

Every.

Last.

One.

"I'm waiting, Serena."

Closing her eyes, Serena took a deep breath and opened her mouth to speak. But when no sound sprang from her parted lips, she clutched at her throat, watching Aramis as realization sank in. The queen's eyes widened, a look of pure shock spreading across her regal features.

"You can't speak?" she whispered. Serena gave a nod, allowing the silence to consume them. A knock at the princess's door captured their concentration. Goosebumps pebbling her milky flesh, sprang up on Serena's arms as her attention turned towards the door, watching as it creaked open without her consent.

Pushing her legs against the magic, Serena bolted for the door. Her heart hammered wildly in her chest, threatening to explode from her ribcage. Her breaths came in short puffs, heaving her chest into overdrive. The princess's fingers caressed the cool metal handle, but she was too late. Petar slipped between the doorframe and the door into the chamber. He turned, the stench of ale and tobacco still on his breath and stumbled into the princess, nearly knocking her over.

"Easy does it," Petar slurred, grasping Serena by the forearm. Her heart thumped wildly, each beat climbing into her throat. She wanted to puke, wanted to escape, but neither were options. Bile crept up her esophagus, pooling in Serena's mouth. She winced as she swallowed the bitter liquid, leaving a less than savory aftertaste in her mouth.

Sucking in a ragged breath, Serena concentrated on her brother, her eyes flicking away from his face briefly to see if Aramis was still in plain view. She was gone or at least sheathed in shadows. She had to protect him like he'd saved her. But with Aramis in her chambers, she wasn't sure how much she could do. He was a siren after all, so would her sister harm him?

Turning, Serena gazed upon her brother, watching his sun-kissed calloused hands run through his windswept locks. His face twisted with emotions Serena knew he was holding back, catching painful words on the tip of his tongue.

"I—" he began but lost his words. Letting out an exasperated sigh, Petar rubbed at his face with the palms of his hands, raking them back through his sandy tresses and began again, "I never thought it would come to this."

Serena cocked her head, issuing for him to explain. "Not everyone in this land wants to see ye rise and shine. Some want to see ye fall and bleed red. I couldn't let me own sister fall. I couldn't let ye bleed for the people that crave bloodshed." The princess narrowed her eyes. She still wasn't following, so Petar continued, "But then ye rose too far and some people came for yer blood themselves and I 'ad to protect ye." Closing his eyes, Petar sucked in a breath. Serena wasn't sure what all of his mumbling was about, just that she had to get him out. Walking to his side, she patted his arm. His eyes snapped open, burrowing into hers. "Get yerself together, Petar," he grumbled to himself over and over again. Serena felt something within her shatter. She felt her brother's desperation call to her like nectar to a bee. And if she felt it… Aramis did too. "I summoned the sea witch." Suddenly everything Serena felt at that moment went icy cold. Her veins froze with fear. No one summoned Ursulana unless they wished death to all.

"Either you're naïve or a complete dunderhead," Aramis replied, her cool voice slicing through the icy chill in the chamber. "So, what did you ask our dear aunt?" Stepping from the shadows, Aramis revealed herself. Serena gulped, her secret divulged, and watched Petar as his jaw unhinged and fell open.

"Ye," he whispered, his eyes raking her body.

"Yes, me," she replied. "Thank you for the coat, though I don't think I'll add it to my courtly attire. Now, enough small talk," Aramis said. "What did you ask for when you summoned Ursulana?"

"I didn't ask her meself."

"Then who, pray tell, did?" Serena's mouth went dry as she watched her sister cross her arms over her ample chest. This was all too much. Averting his gaze, the captain let out a sigh.

"Speak," Aramis commanded. Magic surged within the room, raising the hairs on the back of Serena's neck, beckoning for answers. Petar could fight it, but in the end, the siren queen's words would call to his blood and bring her the answers she desired.

"The slayer." Aramis rose one thin eyebrow at Petar's response before probing further. Her lips quirked into a knowing, nasty grin.

"And what did she ask for?"

"Death," Petar grit out. A muscle feathered in his jaw as he fought against Aramis's hold.

"And how did she seal such a thing?"

"With a kiss," he snarled out. Petar's attention flashed back to Serena. "Serena, did ye kiss Prince Aaron?"

"What does it matter if she did?" Aramis hissed.

"Because if Serena kissed Aaron, death has struck her," Petar sneered back. Serena was tired and growing irritated by the pressing minutes. She was tired of the games and the magic and the riddles between her siblings.

Broken, the voice in her head whispered once more.

"In what way?" Aramis pressed, pulling the answers out of Petar and snapping Serena out of her head.

"What's one way to render a siren defenseless?" Petar posed. Aramis's lip curled as her nose wrinkled.

"Besides surrounding themselves in the company of Mer slum?" A cheap shot if Serena knew one. Petar cocked a brow but remained silent, not giving into the queen. He held eye contact with the her.

Broken.

Broken.

Broken.

"By taking their… oh gods!" Serena watched as realization hit her sister like a ton of bricks. Her pale complexion drained of what little color it had left.

"You will *fix* this. Or so help me, I will tear you apart limb from bloody—"

"I'll fix this. But I might need yer help," Petar replied like the badass he was. He may have ruined Serena's entire life, but she'd be damned if he didn't try to fix it.

MYSTIC

o. No. No. Mystic winced, fighting against the pain in her hardened belly as her uterus contracted. The baby was coming, which was impossible and she was absolutely terrified. She'd been pregnant for two weeks! But now the baby was coming? How could this be?

Magic. She could feel it thrum within her womb, within her veins, and into her unborn child.

Pressure consumed Mystic's lower half, bringing the slayer to her knees. She had to make it to the docks, to her crew. They could get a message to Petar and surely someone would know what to do.

Right?

Right?

Right?!

A scream of pain erupted from her lungs as another contraction took hold of her. Mystic closed her eyes and dug her fingers into the coarse, wet sand and grabbed onto anything she could grasp until the pain passed. Sweat beaded the pirate's brow as she moved one hand to clutch the demon child within her.

"Get. Out. Of. Me," she rasped before another scream escaped her lips. She was better than this. Stronger than this. But yet, she knew she couldn't do this on her own. She needed Petar. She needed him to hold her hand and brush the sweaty curls from her face. She needed to hear him tell her that everything would be okay. She had to get to the docks, to Petar, to—

Footsteps crunched close by, but the tears in her eyes shrouded the guest. Mystic couldn't make out the form as one by one the steps grew louder.

"The sea and the land join as one," the visitor crooned, taking up a spot next to the slayer. She knew that voice. Knew the evil that held that voice captive.

The sea witch.

"Shut up," Mystic hissed. "Shut up and get away from me." Another scream tore from the slayer into the dusk. Tears sprang from her eyes, an involuntary reaction to the pain in her lower half. "Get me to the damned castle!" Mystic hissed. Ursulana's lips perked upwards into a sinister grin as she knelt down next to the pirate.

"I don't take orders from mortals, *mortal*," was all she said before another contraction ripped through Mystic. Her lips parts as she screamed again and again. Her entire body shook. Sweat drenched her skin, clinging her clothes to her. Hot, sticky fluid flowed down her leg, soaking the cloth of her trousers. Mystic sucked in a breath and removed her hand from her belly and parted her thighs. Blood slicked her fingers. Her worst fears coming true.

"It won't be long before the child tears itself free," the sea witch crooned, staring into Mystic's own very tired eyes. "And then the kingdom as you know it will end."

Screw the crew.
 She needed Petar now or she would die.
They all would.

AARON

$\mathcal{A}$aron slammed his shot glass back, relishing the amber liquid as its sweet burn grazed his lips and throat. His mind soared away from Andover and all of his troubles. Away from the meeting his father had called upon him. He wasn't too keen on such affairs where his father was concerned, after all, how could he trust a man who had lied to him his entire life? Treated him like a trophy rather than an heir. He pounded the glass onto the bar, his senses coming back to him as his ears blared with the sudden fiddles of the Lower town tavern. Aaron flicked his wrist, watching the murky shot glass whiz across the bar to the barkeep, a pudgy gentleman with a dark thinning hairline and mustache, who had a worn towel to clean the grime off the glass. The barkeep wore a plain shirt made of wool and dark stained trousers. Aaron wrinkled his nose in disgust, watching as the foam from a previous drink smeared around the glass brim. This was not a place a prince should be and Aaron knew that, but was too drunk to care.

"'Nother?" the barkeep snorted, taking in Aaron's

inebriated state. Aaron fished his hand into his pocket and pulled out a handful of golden coins and thrust them at the bar. He rose to his wobbly feet and pushed past patrons entering the establishment through the worn wooden door. The cool summer's air should have been sobering, but Aaron's vision danced in twos as he took to the cobblestoned path. He walked boot heel to boot heel with his arms out to his sides for balance. Passersby stared, but he paid them no mind until he came to the path that crossed through the docks.

He could hear a woman crying and stopped, staring in the direction of the wails. His eyes traveled to the docks, inspecting every ship that sat anchored in the still port. Nothing was out of the ordinary, and yet, the cries of a woman in pain permeated the night. Aaron turned his attention towards the beach, just south of the docks, and saw two figures hunched in the sand. Nightfall had begun to take hold, casting shadows as the sun dipped below the horizon, but it wasn't dark enough to shroud the women. Aaron's eyes widened as he took in the sight of the slayer, he'd fired a few weeks back. She sat crouched in damp sand. Seawater crashed into her, soaking her from head to toe, and next to her, sat Camilla. Her lavender skirts were sodden, but the marquess didn't seem to notice as her mouth whispered words Aaron couldn't hear. Aaron's heart leapt in his chest, and although he was starting to fall for Serena, he still loved Camilla Delarose with his entire heart. He staggered forward towards the pair, his foot catching on a stone, and turned down the dirt path worn by many before in his current drunken stupor.

Aaron could hear Camilla whispering, but her words were lost to the waves as they came into shore. His boots sunk into the sand with each step, slowing the prince down.

His eyes locked on Mystic's. Tears welled in her widened eyes, streaming down her face as she mouthed, *Run.*

Run? Why would he run?

Hell, he couldn't in this state even if he'd tried. Aaron pushed closer.

"No," Mystic whimpered. "No…" but her crying trailed off into sobs.

"Mystic," Aaron slurred out, reaching the pair. Camilla, to his left, turned, her face oddly calm.

"The baby is coming," Camilla's singsong voice rang as another wave crashed to shore, soaking the foot of Aaron's boots. "We need help. Are you the father?" Aaron craned his neck at his ex-fiancé.

"Really, Cam? You think that low of me?"

"I only meant—" she began, shaking her head, but Aaron held up his palm to her, slicing the words from her tongue. He could feel his magic rolling beneath the surface, even in his current state. His hand tingled with magic, begging to be released.

"Enough," he snapped as nightfall crept in on the dusk. "I don't want to hear you speak. I didn't wish these circumstances either, believe me. But to sit and accuse me of being promiscuous. Just… don't." With that, he turned on his heel and headed back towards the cobblestone road. Mystic let out another howl when Aaron called back over his shoulder, "I'll send Petar. *He's* the father."

THE BABY WAS COMING, WHATEVER THAT MEANT. AARON knew that the women in his life often overreacted. Mystic was showing, but he didn't think she was large enough for birth, not yet at least. It had only been a couple of weeks since Petar and Mystic had gotten together—not enough time for her to be far along if it was even his friend's child. He shook his head and chuckled, imagining the look on his best friend's face when he told him that he was going to be a father, oh, and that his kid was on the way. The reaction is what he craved. To see the pirate he called his best friend, stunned like Aaron often was. His mind was sober by the time he reached the castle gates, nodding to the guards dressed in scarlet tunics adorned in gold metals that gleamed as he passed. They bid him formal greetings, dipping their heads low as they removed their black bear skinned hats and uttered, "Your Highness" before returning to their stoic stances, backs straight, legs stiff, with their arms held behind their backs. Aaron stopped and looked to the guard on his left.

"Clifton," he said gruffly, watching as the guard's eyes locked onto his own. "Send word to Petar that his wench is blubbering down in the docks. Tell him to retrieve her and that she sends a message 'the baby is coming'. Then send word to me. I'll be in the throne room with my father, discussing matters."

Clifton nodded. "Yes, Your Grace," he said and disappeared into the shadows, taking one of the many hidden passages that ran in and out of the castle. Stifling a loose breath, Aaron nodded and bid the guard to his right a good eve and pushed towards the large double doors that greeted him. He needed to meet with his father to discuss wedding details and the affair was likely to be bleak.

THE MEETING IN QUESTION HAD BEEN CALLED IN HIS father's chambers instead of his usual throne room. An oddity for the king, but Aaron didn't examine it further. He didn't know his father, really *know* him. He'd been lying to

Aaron for years. Pushing himself up staircase after staircase, he came to his father's chambers and pushed open the red oak door. His room was nothing special. A hearth that crackled with fire, a dining room adorned with food on a small table and a bed chamber and bathing room. It was much smaller than Aaron remembered, devoid of anything belonging to his mother. Candelabras lit the room, littering the floor and mantle. A fire hazard if Aaron had ever seen one. The king was sat at the dining room table, shoveling custard cake into his bulging cheeks as Aaron approached. He took a seat in the chair across from his father and motioned for the chambermaids to bring him a goblet of wine.

"Things have been set for your wedding to the Adrellan princess," King Marlow boomed, slugging back his goblet of wine. Aaron rolled his eyes, grabbing for a sugared tart, picking at its flaky crust.

"She has a name."

"Yes, yes. Whatever," Marlow replied, shoving another forkful of cake into his mouth.

"It's not whatever, Father," Aaron snapped. "If she is to be the queen of this realm then—"

"Queen? Ha!" King Marlow laughed. "That creature is not fit to sit upon my throne."

"Then why are you forcing this marriage down my throat!" Aaron hissed. "I could have been with Camilla, not gallivanting through town with a fish!"

"Nonsense," King Marlow replied. "You will marry the siren. Andover needs Adrella's forces if we are to push into the other kingdoms. King Bellamy has already pushed into the Forest of Broken Souls. With the dwarves on his side, it is only a matter of time before they attack Andover. We need backup and we will defend our home. So, you will marry the fish girl. Understood?"

"Serena is only next in line for the throne. Why marry me off to the second-best when I could marry a queen?"

"Aramis has taken to a female lover. She has no interest in bearing an heir, thus the throne goes to her sister when the queen passes. You will bear your seed to her and the land and sea will come together as one. Am I understood, boy?"

"What about forces from Alcovera or Swallow Hallow? Why have you not beseeched them for assistance?"

"Swallow Hallow wishes to stay neutral in our conquests and Alcovera has already sent us as many ships as they can without affecting the trade routes and further military forces. We need Adrella's numbers. Do you understand, boy?"

"Perfectly," Aaron ground out. "When is this wedding to come to fruition?"

"Day after 'morrow. Then you will consummate. When an heir is provided, then and only then, will I step down from the throne."

"And should an heir not be born, then what?"

"Oh, there will be an heir. I have no worries about that. Now go ready yourself how you see fit. Preparations for your joining have begun!"

PETAR

etar's lungs burned as he bolted down staircase after staircase, his legs begging for him to rest as he came to and passed landing after landing. His child was coming! Although Mystic hadn't been pregnant long, his time was now. He prayed silently for a boy, someone to carry on his name and bloodline. Of course, if his child turned out to be a girl, he supposed that wouldn't be so bad either. He sprinted until he rounded the last railing and bound for the front gates.

Serena ran behind him, hurdling herself over the edge of the railings only to land down next to him. He turned, her chest heaving as she clutched at her knees, sucking down gulps of air. Petar's eyes darted to her right hand, the hand he was about to grasp and run for the gates. He didn't know if he would be punished for taking Serena beyond the gate without Aaron's permission, but in that moment, he didn't give a rat's arse. He moved swiftly and grasped the siren's supple hand within his own and pulled. He could feel her body resist behind him but pushed forward bounding towards the gate.

Two guards were present, Clifton, the one who had informed him about Mystic and another one that he did not recognize. They stood stoic before him, glancing only briefly at the pirate as he lurched through the gates.

The evening air was cool against his skin, biting and nipping at his exposed flesh like a lover at play. Petar shivered, but the wailing in the distance tore his thoughts away from the cold. Petar knew the fastest way to the port, but towing his sister, that wasn't an option. She would slow him down unless she climbed into his arms. He did not want to go alone. He wasn't stupid. Mystic would need help and he wouldn't be the one to cut the cord.

Petar turned towards his sister, her face flushed and chest rolling; her breaths in gasps. "Get into my arms," he demanded. Time was not on their side. It did not stand still as they stood outside the castle. Another wail in the distance told him that the time for his child was nearing. Serena opened her mouth to object but swiftly shut it.

"That's me child, please!" Petar nearly begged. He could see the defeat in his sister, the utter exhaustion that consumed her body and emanated from her soul. Serena's shoulders slumped as Petar bent down and scooped up the princess. His eyes met hers before she rested her head against his chest. She was light, her body nothing more than skin, bones, and taut muscles. Her nightshirt clung to her, hiking up around her thighs and drooped into the space between her legs. Serena's arms wrapped around her brother's neck, holding tightly.

"Hold on tight now," Petar said and pushed into a sprint.

MYSTIC

*M*ystic howled as claws gripped at her insides, tears pushing through muscle and flesh. Her eyes bore tears, her skin saturated with salt and sea as waves crashed into the shoreline. She was thankful for nightfall, not roasting like the sun, adding insult to injury.

Footfalls sounded in the distance; the ports quiet aside from the occasional ship's bell that rang in the distance. She was alone. Utterly and completely alone with a monster and about to bring her child into the world. Her monster of a child. The footsteps grew closer, slowing as Petar came into view. His face a mask, revealing nothing to the slayer.

Something like joy gripped at her chest, a swell of light in the impending doom that laid before her. She turned to face the sea witch that sat close by, waiting for her to perish, waiting for a spectacle of blood and gore to enchant her. Ursulana's lips curled into a knowing smile as Mystic laid upon the sand, her body growing numb as the cold sliced into her.

"We had a deal," Mystic grit out between contractions. Ursulana tilted her head back, releasing a guttural laugh, not noticing as Serena and Petar crept down the banks from the road. Trees hid them within their shadows. Mystic's gaze darted quickly to meet her beloved's, halting him and Serena in place.

"We did, indeed. You wished for death. But, my dear, you failed to specify in words to whom you wished death upon. So," the sea witch's grin grew wider, "I took your request liberally. I enhanced your pregnancy a tad bit to allow our sweet little morsel to tear herself free. Death will come soon to your poor unfortunate soul, dearie. And once you're nothing but a rotting corpse, then I will kill the prince, the king, and that wretched siren and take the land for myself."

"You're nothing but a demon that I should have slain."

"Should have, could have, would have. The semantics of it all is such a bore. If you think that all monsters are things of folk tales and bumps in the night, perhaps you ought to look more closely at yourself." The witch's words rang through the slayer's ears, hanging in the air.

Fire burned within Mystic's belly as tears rolled from her eyes. Her bones began to crack and crunch and her belly began to viciously move. Silently, she prayed for the Fates to cut her strand, for her death to be swift and painless, but as her body rumbled with life and magic, Mystic knew she wouldn't be so lucky.

"You will die a painful death and feel every tear and crack that child brings you in the name of our kin you have slain. Ironic isn't it? That the slayer will be slain from her hybrid babe?"

"Shut—" Mystic hissed before a screech tore from her throat, slicing her vocal cords raw. Her vision blurred to black as the fire within erupted. Her insides were outside, spattering her face and hands. Tears rolled down the pirate's cheeks, and a chill ran down her spine, cradling her. Mystic felt her body grow cold, the fire from her belly ceasing and the darkness around her tunnel into the light. She felt calm, at peace as she looked at that light. Her spirit lifted, and she looked down at her eviscerated corpse and felt nothing. Her ears rang, first with a high-pitched noise and then with a song she knew very well.

Come with me and then you'll see
For a child of the sea, you were born to be
Die you must, to join us.
In our haunting melody.

A hand outstretched to Mystic as she lifted her gaze from her body to the owner. A man with long, blonde, curly hair and braided beard stood before her. His body bore nothing more than a wrap that covered his nether region and half of his defined torso. Lightning sprung from his hand, but it did not shock her.

"Come, Daughter. Neverland is waiting."

"But you're…" Mystic said, though her lips did not move.

The man smiled. "I am."

"Zeus," Mystic whispered, her spirit growing warmer in the light.

"Your work here is not yet done. Come, and together we will walk into the Never-Never and then we can talk." Mystic nodded, her lips perking as she took the man's hand and walked into the light.

33

SERENA

Serena watched the light fade from the slayer's eyes and looked to Petar, his body frozen in anger or fear, she did not know. He trembled, setting Serena down as his fists clenched at his sides. Purple blood welled in his palms, dripping into the sand below. Serena moved, racing towards the slayer's cooling corpse, the babe, still attached by the umbilical cord, dying as Ursulana stood and met her gaze.

"And just what do we have here?" she cooed. Serena had no time to think, just react. Her eyes flicked to her brother, trembling with rage as he began to move at inhuman speed.

"You fucking killed me wife!" Petar hollered, launching himself at the sea witch. The pair danced, bobbing and weaving. Each delivering blows that stunned Serena. She shook her head. Her brother was fighting for his baby, who was dying as the seconds passed. Serena bolted towards the mess of blood and bowels spattered along the beach. Serena wrinkled her nose, the stench alone sending bitter bile up her throat. She gulped hard, forcing the liquid back down her throat and plunged her hands into the slayer's belly.

Pulling the baby from the remains, she noticed the cord, and with nothing to cut it with, she held the baby up to her mouth, closed her eyes and clamped down. Her serrated teeth sliced through the cord effortlessly as Serena turned the baby over and patted its backside. The baby let out a wail, filling its lungs with air as she held it close to her body, using her shirt to wrap the baby.

Serena glanced down, noticing the lack of a member between the child's legs and smiled.

A girl.

34

AARON

*A*aron needed an escape from the lands and his duties. The meeting with his father had been unbearable, as he knew it would be. All he wanted to do was to slum in the Lowertown taverns, frequent the outlawed bordellos and board a ship to gods knew where. He was a pawn, nothing more nor less, in his father's games. Aaron cursed at himself. He should have known better, all this time, he should have known. Magic surged within his veins, honing in on release. He needed alcohol, and fast. He needed to numb the magic that thrummed within him and he needed to find the girl in the tower.

She was the key.

Rummaging through his dimly- lit wardrobe, Aaron pulled out a cloak of crushed velvet, the color of wine and blood, embroidered with gold threads. He cherished the cloak, something that had once belonged to his father, a gift handmade by the late queen. He donned the cloak and walked over to one of the many bookcases within his study, pulling back a lever, he watched the shelf slide to the side, revealing one of the many hidden passages that led through the castle. If the king wanted him to prepare, well then damn it, he would.

The passage was dark, full of twists and turns the prince had taken time and time again being drunk, only to sober up quicker than he'd liked. This time was no different. He moved, hands outstretched against the cool stone walls, feeling his way with every twist, turn, and obstacle in his path. Cool light filled the end of the tunnel leading into the courtyard and grand gates. Aaron moved into the tunnel's entrance and pulled out his golden pocket watch, lit only with the light of the full moon. Aaron smiled. The guards would be changing shifts by the time he made it through the courtyards and to the gate.

Pushing himself into the shadows, Aaron dipped in and out of the line of trees towards the gates, reaching them in time to watch the guards move into the closest passage. Their voices echoed off the walls as they spoke to the guards taking over. Aaron peered around corner after corner before pushing through the entrance.

He ran, his cloak billowing behind him as his feet fell upon cobblestones. He just needed to get past the shops, through the port, and into the slums without being spotted. He'd have a drink or ten and then board the *Camilla Delarose* one last time.

PETAR

*P*etar lunged forward, his teeth bared as he swiped his claws at the sea witch. She dodged moving left and right with every blow. Laughter rang through the air, like a taunt of his will. If only he had magic, he could fight fire with fire. Light against dark.

He lunged again, barreling himself into her body, his shoulder driving into her belly. Claws ripped into his back as the pair crashed to the ground. Air whizzed out of Petar's lungs, sending him into a coughing fit as he tried to catch his breath. Pain cracked through his knees but he moved quickly, straddling the witch. Anger suffocated his thinking as Petar punched and slashed, his nails making contact and tearing at the witch's visage. Black goo oozed from her wounds, soaking into the ground beneath them. The witch cackled again, thrusting her forehead into Petar's.

Blinding pain erupted through his head as light danced before his eyes. Petar clamped his eyes shut just for a moment, but Ursulana took the opening, thrusting her knee upward, she made contact with his groin.

Everything hurt as his stomach roiled in pain. Bile and vomit erupted from his mouth as the captain fell to the side. He thought about his baby girl growing up without her mother. He couldn't allow her to be an orphan and silently, in that moment, he vowed to destroy the sea witch. For his daughter. For Mystic.

"Wench," Petar hissed, grabbing for his dagger in one hand and family jewels in the other. Pain seared in his nether region, crippling him. He wanted to move, wanted to fight, but the pain radiating through his body held him prisoner. Ursulana rolled and moved atop the pirate. She outstretched her hand, grasping his neck with her cool fingers.

"Such a pity," she purred, "for your poor, unfortunate soul," and plunged her nails deep within the pirate's windpipe.

AARON

"She's a beaut!" Petar exclaimed running his hand along the deck railing. "What 'er ye gonna name her?" he asked. Aaron had never thought of it. He'd never imagined his father would gift him with a ship.

"The Camilla Delarose, after my Cam," he crooned.

"Are we gonna plunder and loot? I can get ye a crew."

"Nay," Aaron replied. "We're going to decimate sirens."

"Yer a lucky bastard," Petar said. "I'd kill a thousand sirens and settle down, if it meant I get a ship like this." His cerulean eyes widened. Aaron wasn't sure if it was lust or excitement or both that lit his best friend's face, but he liked the look on Petar.

"Be my Cap'n?" Aaron blurted. Petar's body grew still.

"Really?"

"Aye, really. Get a crew and we'll voyage at first light." Petar's lips spread into the largest grin Aaron had ever seen.

"Ye have yerself a cap'n."

AARON'S HEART HAMMERED IN HIS CHEST, THREATENING TO explode. His magic thrummed with life as his legs begged for him to slow his pace. His breaths came in ragged little puffs and sweat slicked his skin and brows. Cries greeted the prince's ears as he rounded alley after alley, dipping in and out of the shadows. He was so close to the port. So close to the taverns, when the beach came into view.

His body slowed. His reality lurching to a halt as he took in Camilla's bloodied body. Terror froze him in place as she cackled in the sand below.

Petar squirmed beneath her grip, but it was no use. Camilla crouched overtop of his best friend and smiled as though she knew he was watching before she tore out Petra's throat. Everything around the prince went still. His ears rang. He wanted to scream, to beat the living daylights out of his ex-lover, but instead, he stood there in the alley, his body thrumming. Another image of Petar flashed though his mind.

"'Is not so bad," Petar grumbled as Aaron's healer tended to the gash in his side. Purple blood tricked from the wound, but Aaron was too preoccupied to notice the warning signs that his friend was something else entirely.

"That beast almost got the best of you. What do you mean it's not so bad!"

"'Tis only a cut, Aaron. But did ye see how scared the sea scum was when I pulled him aboard?"

"Aye. But he was already half-dead. Something or someone tried to kill him."

"He said his name was Calix."

"Who cares, he's dead and almost killed you in the process. I don't know what I'd do if I ever had to watch you die. Don't think I could handle such a thing," Aaron said, pulling a flask of rum from his pocket. He handed the booze to his friend, who took a swig before the healer began to stitch him up.

"Don't ye worry. Nothing will best me."

Aaron moved, without knowledge and without recollection, from the shadows. Sand crunched beneath his feet and the area around him glowed with light.

"*Kaló vrontí.*" I summon thunder. Wind whipped Aaron's face and body as the clouds above swirled. Thunder boomed and lightning crackled, supercharging his body. His hands tingled, singing to the clouds as he raised up his right hand. "*Astrapí,*" he spat.

Camilla turned; her face amused. "Cute," she sneered. "But a princeling like you knows nothing of the gods." Aaron felt his cheeks widen into a grin as a bolt of lightning struck directly into his hand. He wielded the power and pulled back his arm, the lightning danced up, surrounding his shoulder and down his torso as he launched the bolt direct at Camilla.

Her eyes grew to orbs, fear etching her face as the bolt penetrated her right through the heart.

"Die, bitch," Aaron hissed, before dropping like a rock to the bottom of the ocean.

Magic rose from the witch, a dark veil rising as if to protect her body and cracked, releasing Serena's voice into the open. Camilla's husk shattered into hundreds of black eels just as waves crashed against the shore. Water engulfed the creatures, sucking them back out to sea.

PETAR

Petar gripped at his neck, his hands filling with hot sticky blood as the purple liquid oozed from his gaping wound. He was dying, there was no escaping that. He sucked in a ragged breath, wincing. His lungs burned, everything burned and he was dying.

What?

Darkness clouded the edges of his vision, tunneling. The end was coming and yet, here he was. The captain sighed, relieving the pressure threatening to burst forth from his lungs. He tried to move his head, but it felt so heavy as the darkness grew. Someone was touching him; their touch was like a feather against his skin as his body grew heavy.

"Petar," Serena sobbed. He moved his eyes to look at her, but his gaze fell short as the tunnel of light moved further away. Petar opened his mouth to speak, choking and coughing. The taste of copper flooded his tongue and taste buds.

"Shh, don't speak," Serena pleaded. But he had to. He

had to let her know that he loved her. He had to have her save his daughter from Ursulana.

"Pppppp-ee-tttttra," he gurgled. Something warm hit his face. Tears, he supposed. It was the only logical answer. He already felt his blood draining from him, so he knew it wasn't that.

"She'll be safe. I promise," Serena replied, her voice shaking and weak. He knew he shouldn't give into Death, shouldn't leave his daughter to grow up as an orphan. A chill consumed his body. "She'll be safe," he heard again as the dark abyss grew around him. Petar knew that this was it. There would be no happy endings for him. No last goodbyes. No kisses or hugs or slaps on the back. His last voyage was upon him. Alone. Petar wanted to speak, wanted to tell Serena he was sorry for missing years with her. To tell her how proud he was of her and how much she'd grown. He wanted to be there to walk her down the aisle to his best friend, but that would never come to pass. A shiver wracked his body, freezing him to the core.

"Let go, Petar. She will be safe. Let go and fly away to Neverland," his sister whispered. He felt her lips graze his forehead as the darkness consumed his vision. Petar's chest heaved a final breath as the light grew from the tunnel. A figure stood before Petar, shrouding their face from him. Warmth flooded the pirate, enveloping him like that of an old friend.

"Come with me Petar," the woman said.

"Mystic?" he asked, though his voice sounded far away. The woman nodded and smiled as her appearance formed before him.

"Come with me Petar and together we will fly to a place where the darkness cannot touch us. Where we will never grow old. Never die. We can live the life we were meant to have together." Petar felt his spirit lift as the light grew. Mystic stood, unscathed and smiled, a true smile. She outstretched her hand towards him. Her beautiful hand.

"I can't leave Petra behind. She needs 'er father."

"She is in the best hands I can think of, my sweet. But you're not. Come with me." Petar hesitated, looking back down at his body and let out a breath.

"I'm coming, me love," he said, grasping her fingers within his own. Together, they turned and faced the light, allowing it to consume them until the pain and sadness and tears were no more.

SERENA

Shattered.

Broken.

Her body was numb as she laid Petra down beside her cooling mother's corpse and stood. Her legs were shaky but strong enough for her to get to Aaron before collapsing. Her hands felt foreign as she fumbled to pull his head into her lap. Tears streamed down her milky cheeks, dripping from her nose into the sand below.

"Don't leave me," she sobbed. "Aaron, I need you. Please." Her voice was raw, stinging her throat. "I need you," she whispered, cradling Aaron's head to her chest. Coos from the baby sounded near Mystic, settling Serena's soul. She couldn't raise her niece on her own. She couldn't. She—

Aaron's eyes fluttered. He inhaled what Serena imagined was the scent of the sea, salt, shit, and death, and pushed himself into a sitting position. He looked normal, but Serena had seen him wield Zeus's power. She gulped, her body still trembling and without hesitation, pulled Aaron into a kiss. Her eyes closed, relishing in the softness of his mouth, the flick of his tongue against her lips, begging her to let him in. Their lips melded together, moving in rhythm with one another, fast and fervent. Serena grasped Aaron's face, holding him closer to her as she opened her mouth to let him in. She needed him. Aaron moaned and knotted his fingers in the siren's ruby locks, before pulling away.

"You're all I've got now," he said, staring into Serena's bright eyes. She was the glue holding the cracked walls of the prince together and someday her prince would shatter and there would be no fix.

"And Petra," Serena replied, pushing to her feet. Her fingers wrapped around his, pulling him upright. Wrapping an arm around Serena, the prince leaned his weight on the siren.

"Petra?" Aaron asked, arching his brow.

"My niece. The true heir to the Adrellan throne." Aaron's eyes widened as he realized what she was saying.

"True heir?"

"Yes, I'll explain later. Besides, I never wanted the throne, anyway."

"Heed your words," Aaron whispered.

"Can you stand?" Serena asked, her gaze flicking towards Mystic's corpse.

"I can damn sure try." Unfurling the prince's arm from her neck, Serena moved away taking one careful step after another. "I'm fine," Aaron called out, nodding towards Petra. Serena sucked in a deep breath and crouched down, scooping the baby into her arms as a large wave crashed into the slayer. Serena looked down at her still niece, watching her chest rise and fall before turning to look at Aaron. She returned to his side and wrapped the baby closer to her.

"Come on," Aaron said, "We need to get her back to the castle. And then you and I need to talk."

S ERENA SAT WITH HER LEGS FOLDED BENEATH HER IN A RED crushed velvet armchair in Aaron's chambers. He'd lent her a tunic to cover her naked form, tossing the tattered shirt she'd had into the hearth. She held her sleeping niece close to her chest, nestled in several woolen blankets, fighting off the chill that threatened their bones. Fire crackled from the hearth before them, its orange glow casting shadows around the dimly lit room. Above the dark mantle hung a large painting of a ship sailing rough waters. Hues of blues and greens melded together, reminding Serena briefly of her home. To the right of the hearth, stood a short table and in front of that table, stood Aaron with his white linen back to her. He sighed and turned towards Serena, his dark eyes sparkling in the fire's light.

"Care for a drink?" he asked. In his left hand, he held a small crystallized glass with mahogany liquid sloshing around its sides.

"I don't know how you can drink that awful stuff," she replied, wrinkling her nose, before lowering her gaze to Petra. She had her father's nose and ears, but her mother's skin tone and mouth. She didn't know whose eyes she had.

"Alcohol takes off the edge, numbs the pain, quiets the magic and the insufferable reality we live in. Don't you ever get bored?"

"Not lately," Serena replied. Her mind whirled of what to do next. She had to tell Aaron everything, every last dirty detail. They were in this together. They had to be.

Aaron plopped into the chair next to her, tearing the siren from her rambling thoughts and swirled drink.

"So," he began. Serena looked up. Aaron's eyes were locked onto her. Her lips parted to speak, but something fluttered in her stomach.

"We have a lot to talk about and the dawn approaches us in a few hours."

Serena cleared her throat. "Yes. Right. So, where to begin?" she said aloud, watching the embers turn from yellow to orange to red.

"Serena?"

"Hmm?" Rubbing her eyes with the back of her hand, she fought to regain her thoughts. Sleep beckoned her and she so desperately wanted to give in.

"Dawn approaches and with it, chaos. My best friend is dead. Mystic, too. Broken bodies lay on the beach with blood spattered everywhere. We have this kid that we have no idea what to do with and I have about a thousand bloody questions. You said you had things to discuss and I'm hoping we can get a few of those answered before the castle wakes. Now, hand me the baby and start from the beginning." Serena's lips perked upwards as she maneuvered her niece into the crook of the prince's arms. Petra moved slightly but remained asleep. Aaron smiled as he looked into the child's face and Serena, fighting back a yawn, began her tale.

"Our kingdoms were at war, a long and bloody one. My father was losing, so he sent my eldest sister, Ophelia, to gather intel from a year on the land. A year that continued in bloodshed for both sides. When Ophelia returned home, her body couldn't recover from its time spent above the sea. Day by day, her strength dwindled and with it, my father's sanity. Not long after she returned home, Ophelia died and with her, a part of my father.

Stricken by grief, my father took to the land to command his armies and got himself killed."

"And Aramis took the throne?" Aaron asked, his voice quiet. Serena nodded.

"Yes. But my sister isn't who you think she is. She's not kind nor just. She seeks power. When our father and sister died, her heart filled with hatred and she spent the better part of a year devising a plan to get her revenge on Andover.

"Upon her coronation, she met with your father and agreed to call back the troops. Told him that the war was meaningless and gave your sailors safe passage through the Adrellan Pass in exchange for you and me to wed, under your father's conditions. Your father obliged my sister's idiotic request, but Aramis never intended to have you and I marry. She commanded me to kill you and your father. At the time, her command pushed me to find you, made me suffer that transformation and stow upon your ship with you and your crew. But then I met Petar." Aaron's body tensed as if the sound of his friend's name shattered his soul. His eyes danced, fighting back tears that escaped and rolled down his cheeks, pushing him to a place she knew he didn't want to visit.

"Petar, may he rest in peace," Aaron whispered.

"May he rest in peace," Serena replied before continuing her story. "Petar's blood sang to me. He was a siren. He was my brother, the true heir of Adrella, though at the time I hadn't known. Not until he saved me that day from drowning."

"Wait, what? So, you're telling me that my best friend was really my enemy?"

"Yes, I guess in a way I am."

"Son of a—" he cut off, pinching the bridge of his

nose between his thumb and forefinger. "So, on the day you almost drowned, why didn't you transform back?"

"I started to, but the ascension didn't take. I think it's because my destiny is to be with you, here," Serena said. Blood rushed to her cheeks. She cleared her throat and focused her attention on the painting that hung above the mantle.

"So, here I was on ship with my brother and the prince, ordered to deliver a death blow. At first, I wanted nothing more than to feel your blood seep between my fingers, but you had the slayer aboard and well, I valued my life too much.

"Then we came into port and you taught me your ways and showed me a kindness, I was so unaccustomed to. So, I decided to let you live. But that wasn't good enough for my sister. She came to Andover to check up on me and found out that I had lost my voice."

"Does she still expect you to kill me?" Aaron interrupted, shifting uncomfortably in his seat.

"If I don't, then she likely will," Serena replied. From the corner of her eye, she saw Aaron's throat bob as he swallowed hard. He shifted Petra in his arm and placed a hand on the hilt of a hidden dagger.

"And are you going to murder me?" he asked, his voice remaining low.

"No," Serena replied, watching as Aaron's brows furrowed. Confusion etched across his handsome features, wrinkling the lines in his forehead.

"Why not?" he asked, his body relaxing slightly. "Not that I want to die, but why would you risk it?"

"Because I've grown to care for you, Aaron, and we're in this together."

The fire crackled between the pair as both looked elsewhere, remaining quiet.

"Tomorrow we're to be married before the kingdom. Are you ready for that?" Aaron asked before reaching with his free hand for his drink. He tipped back his head and downed the entire glass before resting the empty crystal upon his pant leg.

"With you, this world doesn't seem so bad," Serena said as she watched the fire die. "With you, I'll be as ready as I can be."

Serena awoke in a daze, her neck and back stiff and aching from sleeping in the chair. Aaron sat next to her with Petra nestled quietly against his chest. She hadn't made a sound. Pushing herself upright, Serena stretched before getting to her feet. The room was still dark, but from the sounds outside the prince's chambers, she assumed it to be mid-morning. No knocks had come to the prince's door. No disturbance in the world.

Her legs strained and knees popped as she stood upright. Slowly, the princess moved in front of Aaron, both hands shaking as she reached out to take Petra from his body. Petra's eyes fluttered open, staring at Serena with a knowing look. Something was different about her niece, something Serena couldn't place, but she had no time to ponder that.

Setting Petra down upon her cooling chair, Serena rushed to Aaron's wardrobe, pulling a dark wool cloak from its hanger and drew it over top of her. She rushed back and scooped Petra swiftly to her chest before quietly tiptoeing to the door. She had one shot to get to her chambers without being discovered, and one person she could trust to watch Petra with her life while Serena sold her soul to Andover.

Yellow Teeth.

Serena's skin was slick with a thin layer of sweat as she ran, ducking in and out of the shadows of the corridors. Beads of sweat brimmed her brow, slowly trailing a line to her burning eyes. Her breaths came in strained, uneven puffs and her chest heaved heavily. She tried to get a hold of herself, calm her nerves before she gave herself away. Serena knew she shouldn't be in this section of the castle, let alone seen coming out of the prince's chambers on their wedding day.

Tomorrow will be different, she thought. *Tomorrow we can take the world by storm.* There was still so much to discuss with Aaron and the scheme to be made. Tomorrow, she reminded herself.

Swallowing hard, Serena rounded corner after corner, making sure to steer clear of the servants and chambermaids, holding Petra close to her chest. She let out an audible sigh as she spotted her chamber door and thrust it open.

"Where have you been?" Yellow Teeth hissed as she crossed the room towards Serena. "Have you any idea what preparations we have today? Have you any care, Serena?" Serena cast her gaze towards the floor.

"I'm sorry," she said quietly. "But I need a favor from you." She lifted her eyes and met Yellow Teeth's widened ones. Quickly but quietly, Yellow Teeth loosened her arms and crossed the chamber, closing the large door.

"Now," she said, "what type of favor can the future queen request? And what will ol' Kinsley get in return?"

"Who is Kinsley?"

"Why, me, miss." Why hadn't she known Yellow

Teeth's real name? Why hadn't she asked? Serena's mind raced with question after question. But she didn't have time to ponder them. Serena swallowed, and with her index finger and thumb, undid the clasp on the prince's cloak. It fell to the ground in one fell swoop.

"Where did ye get the wee babe?" Kinsley asked quietly.

"Does it matter?"

"Indeed, it does! I will not be hung in the square for your crimes. Did ye kidnap the child'?"

"More like rescued," Serena countered. "She's my niece and an orphan."

"Blimey!" Kinsley exclaimed, clasping her pudgy fingers over her mouth.

"Will you watch her until Aaron and I can take her as our ward? Watch her for this afternoon, nonetheless?" Serena watched Kinsley drop her hands and a genuine smile creep across her features.

"Oh, give me the babe!" she cried. "And draw yourself a bath. You must be clean for the prince!"

"You know, if I wasn't exhausted, I'd fight you on this," Serena mumbled. "But I think a bath might be just what I need before this day ensues." And with that she walked past her bed and into her bath chambers, slamming the door.

AARON

*A*aron awoke to the sound of crackling firewood as someone tossed another log into the hearth. He rubbed the sleep from his eyes and sat up.

"The princeling lives," an unfamiliar female voice stated. Aaron blinked, focusing on the woman and taking in her delicate features. Her hair was long and dark, draped down her left shoulder in a slew of curls. A fringed tiara of crystals and diamonds glittered from atop her head. Her dark eyes bore a similar likeness to Serena's in shape, that Aaron couldn't deny. His breath hitched in his throat.

Aramis.

"And to what do I owe the Queen of Adrella's presence on this joyous day?" he asked. His heart beat faster, but he had to remain calm. Aramis's eyes glistened in the firelight as she took a step closer to the prince. Aaron's eyes shifted down her dark blue bodice and skirts, adorned with gems of sapphire and diamonds that sent shards of light glittering across the floorboards. She was breathtaking.

"Joyous day?" her shrill voice jeered. Dread coursed

through Aaron's veins, his heart hammering and a cool chill crept down his spine. His stomach knotted and his magic tingled. He could feel it in every nerve of his body, singing to him. Aramis took another step forward. "I'd hardly say your wedding day is a joyous day."

"Why? Because I'm supposed to be dead?" Aaron spat. Aramis's lips rose into a slight smirk.

"Exactly," she purred. "You're going to come with me, alive, and in return for your life, you're going to give me your kingdom." A laugh trickled up the prince's throat. It was never his kingdom to give.

"And should I refuse?" he asked, watching as the queen took several more steps towards him.

"Then I'll show no mercy." Aaron bit at his lip, stifling back the laughter in his throat. The queen could threaten him all she'd like, but he had defeated the sea witch and he would defeat her too. Rising to his feet, Aaron stood more than a foot taller than the queen and her diadem. His fingers balled into fists as he thrust his hands into the pockets of his trousers. He flicked his tongue across the bottoms of his upper teeth before his lips perked into a grin he could no longer hide.

"I'm not going with you. And you're not going to fight me," he replied.

"Oh, you're going," a voice crooned from behind, pushing a blade into Aaron's back.

"Did you really think I'd come here alone?"

"I didn't think—" Aramis held up her hand cutting Aaron off.

"That was rhetorical. I don't give a damn what you think, human," Aramis hissed. "Shay, use any force necessary to bring him to Adrella. Do keep him alive. When we hit the water, bind him with it so that he can breathe. Mortals are so very fragile, aren't they?"

SERENA

erena looked around, confusion washing through her as the stench of death filtered through her nostrils. A scent she hadn't smelled since that day on the ship. She was in a long hall, one that she knew very well, adorned in gold pillars and creamy white walls. Tapestries of red and gold hung from the stones behind a golden throne. Drapes of blood-red hung between pillars. Candelabras were lit amongst table after table littered with food as far as the eye could see. Faceless men and creatures sat at the tables all wearing suits of Andoverian armor as they picked at stuffed turkeys and honeyed yams, laughing and howling. But despite the food that sat upon the tables, the smell of filth and death stung Serena's nose. She turned in place, wondering how the tables were now behind her. Something hot and wet flowed through her fingers as she approached the dais. Serena glanced down, her stomach lurching as blood ran down her wrists. She wanted to wipe it away, but her attention waned as she took a step up onto the platform. A small creature in white stood with her back to Serena. Her skirts billowed though there was no breeze. Serena's stomach knotted as she reached a hand out and clasped it upon the small creature's shoulders. The creature turned and Serena gasped.

Blood poured from its mouth, saturating the white dress and staining its cocoa skin. The princess's eyes darted to the throne and the heap of flesh and bones and blood that piled before it.

Marlow.

The princess's eyes darted back to the creature as it smiled and said, "Hello, Auntie."

Serena jolted awake to screams from the other room. She hadn't realized she'd dozed off in her bath, the water now cold and her skin pruned. She hadn't ascended, not a scale or a tear tarnished her. Pushing from the tub, Serena grabbed for her towel and quickly wrapped it around her, trailing water behind her as she ran for the door. Her fingers fumbled as she gripped the cool handle and turned it, wrenching it open.

Kinsley stumbled backward from Serena's bed as dark tendrils enveloped Petra in a swaddling embrace. Serena took a step towards her niece, her stomach knotting and twisting the closer she got. One step, a punch to the gut. Another step, a twist of fury. Step after grueling step, Serena fought against her human body to get to her bedside and when she was within an arm's length of Petra, the darkness whipped out, faltering her step and rendering her useless. Bones crunched in her right arm as a searing pain shot up to her shoulder. Serena's vision grew white as the pain took over. She shook her head, wishing the pain away, but her human body did not obey, did not mend. The princess turned away from Petra, guilt eating her up inside and pulled her broken arm to her chest, cradling it with her good one. They could only wait. Wait to see if the darkness would fade. Wait to see what became of her brother's child.

She moved back towards Kinsley, who stood shaking in place. Her face ashen and eyes wide as she took in Serena's mangled arm. Had they been alone, Serena knew that Kinsley would have fussed over such injuries, addressing them as she saw fit. But they weren't alone, they were far from it.

Seconds passed to minutes before the shadows that loomed over Petra dissipated, but when they did, there was no longer a baby before them, but a young girl of seven.

Her skin was an even medley of milk and chocolate, rich and warm of color. Her hair was a mess of dark curls like her slayer mother, but her frame and build, long and lean like her father. Serena's jaw dropped, and she heard Yellow Teeth beside her squeak and fall to the floor. A smile played on Petra's lips as she held her arms out, beckoning for an embrace.

"Petra," Serena whispered. "What? How?"

"Magic has a price to pay," Petra began to sing. *"Of blood and sin, we all could say."* Serena's eyes widened. She knew that song, that forbidden melody. But how had this infant child, her niece, known such darkness? *"Nothing in this realm is free."*

"What have you done?" the siren huffed. Screams echoed from the halls and Serena reacted without thinking, pushing herself to the door and whipping it open. She rushed into the hall, grabbing a maiden.

"What's happened?" she asked.

"The king is dead," she replied, tears running down her alabaster cheeks. Dead? But how? And when?

"And Aaron?" Serena pressed on.

"No one has seen him since this morning, my lady."

"Then who is in charge?"

"I guess you are, seeing as you were to be queen today. You best get to the throne room miss, errrm, Your Majesty, Your Highness."

"Serena," she corrected, releasing the maiden and smoothing out the wrinkles of her sleeve. "Thank you," she said and turned back to her room. Her eyes narrowed upon Petra.

"I'll ask again," she snarled. "What have you done?" Petra smiled back, holding her arms behind her and raised to her tiptoes.

"I killed the king," she said matter-of-factly, her tone taking on an innocence the girl was far from. "I killed the king and used his energy."

"And why would you do that? How would you do that?! You were an infant!"

"You needed to be the queen. I made you the queen. What else is there to say?"

"What are you?" Serena snapped. "How did a baby kill the most powerful king the land has seen since Zeus himself?"

"I am magic and all things humans cannot perceive. I am what I am, but more than that, I am Petra."

"What does that even mean!" Serena roared, tossing her hands into the air, then paused. "Never mind, thanks to you I have a kingdom to run." Running to her clothes pile, she fetched the emerald green gown she'd worn only days before. Serena shuffled herself into the gown the best that she could, despite the pain in her arm and bit her lip to stop herself from howling out in pain. Her eyes narrowed on Petra.

"Stay here and don't hurt Kinsley. Oh, and stay out of trouble." Pulling on a pair of boots, Serena ran to the door and set off into the chaos.

SERVANTS SCREAMED AS THEY PUSHED EACH OTHER, running towards stairwells and exits. Serena had gathered her skirts with her good hand and pushed her way into the crowd.

She needed to get to the throne room.

She needed to find Aaron. Rounding corner after corner, taking routes she barely remembered, Serena happened upon a long corridor. A familiar stench slapped her in the face, stopping the siren dead in her tracks. Death and fury and magic hung in the air, gagging Serena. Her stomach twisted as bile stung its way up her throat. The stench was overbearing, death and copper.

Before her sat two large double doors. Serena approached cautiously. Whatever darkness loomed over the land had taken her niece and murdered the king. The princess gulped and pushed open one of the large, heavy doors.

Long tables dressed in gold and silver adorned the hall before the dais, each set for the wedding festivities that were planned for the day. But Serena stared ahead, her feet moving numbly beneath her as she approached the dais. Her eyes widened as she took in the king's crumpled body and the pool of blood seeping out around him. Marlow's golden crown sat askew on his skull. Serena gulped, her breath hitching in her throat.

Lifting her skirts, Serena stepped onto the dais, Marlow's blood sticky and cooling beneath her feet. She dropped her skirts, watching as they soaked up the dark ruby liquid and knelt next to the king's head. Her fingers grazed the cool surface of his crown, lifting it free from his dead skull. Serena stared at the crown and then lifted her gaze to the cool gold throne. Another step, and she was over the late king's corpse. She stood before the throne and turned, lowering herself into it.

Serena looked out upon the room that was supposed to hold a grand party—her union to Aaron—and sighed before looking back at the scrap of gold in her hands. Raising the crown with her good hand, she placed it haphazardly onto her own skull and waited. Grief encompassed her entire being, numbing her to the core. She'd lost everything and everyone she'd grown to care for. Serena's body felt heavy as she sank into the golden throne, remembering every detail from the last two weeks. She'd gained a brother, learned how to love, fallen for a prince, and gained a niece. She'd overcome fear, overcome her hatred, only for her to hurt like she'd never hurt before. Serena swallowed, fighting against the tears that flowed freely from her eyes, dripping onto her chest. But she didn't care. She was empty and lost and alone.

Hours passed and Serena sat staring out into the hall with no one to keep her company but the king's cold corpse. Eventually, someone had come to the throne room, a courtier with a handsome face and a name Serena didn't know. His chest was heaving as though he'd run the entire castle searching for her, which Serena knew was very possible.

"My lady," he huffed, pausing when he spotted the crown on her head.

"Aaron?" she croaked. The first words she'd spoken since Petra transformed in her chambers. Petra, the thought of the girl brought a bitter taste to Serena's mouth as she puckered her lips.

"My lady."

"Queen," Serena corrected.

"My lady," the courtier went on, causing the princess to roll her eyes in dismay. "We have searched the castle high and low for the prince, the rightful heir to the throne, but all we found was this," he said, shoving his hand into his pocket and rifling around. The courtier withdrew a piece of paper and approached the dais. He extended his hand out to Serena, who snatched the paper from his fingers and read silently.

I did what you didn't.
Give me the crown and the throne
Or he dies.

Serena's fingers curled around the paper, fury pulsing through her body as she gritted out, "The prince has been kidnapped." She watched the courtier's eyes widen and his face grow stark white before she continued, "Bind me to the land. Make me officially Queen."

"I-I don't have any say, my lady."

"Then get me someone who does and do it now. Or the prince dies." With that order, she watched as the courtier turned and ran from the throne room, leaving her once again with Marlow and her fury.

Serena's first command was obliged as the council she'd never met, gathered before her in the throne room. Gasps of horror echoed in the air as they each took in the king's corpse and crown upon her head. But after reading the note given to Serena, none of them had objected. They held a coronation in secrecy and would reveal to all of Andover their new queen, come the new day's light. Serena explained she had a charge and then after all explanations were out in the open, Serena retreated to her chamber.

Petra was already asleep, tucked into her bed with Kinsley passed out in a chair next to her. Relief flooded the siren as she took to the other side of the bed. As much as she didn't want to be near her bloody niece, she wanted to sleep in comfort before everything came to light. Stripping her dress from her, Serena pulled on a sleeping gown and pulled back the covers to her bed, nestling with her back to Petra.

She'd sleep with one eye open before she trusted the girl. And come morning, she would find a way to keep her crown and save her love.

EPILOGUE

SERENA

Serena rested her hand upon her niece's caramel shoulders and looked out into the bay. Waves crashed against the shore in unison as the sun set along the horizon. She cleared her throat and looked down at the child before her.

"Do you see the waves?" she asked, before gulping down the lump in her throat. She knew something like this could happen. But never knew it would be under these circumstances and never so soon. To threaten Aaron, to threaten her, Aramis had a lot of nerve. Petra turned, her dark eyes boring into Serena and nodded.

"Good," Serena replied, watching as darkness consumed the sky. "Because you are a beacon of the land and sea, and we will show Adrella that if they mess with the land, they better sleep with one eye open."

"Oh, you have no idea," Petra smirked.

"They have no idea how fast the Dark Tides turn," Serena replied, staring out into the bay.

To be continued...

ACKNOWLEDGMENTS

A big thank you goes out to my two editors, Carol and Maggie for polishing this gem for all of you.. To Zoe Perdita, for the gorgeous map and to Moorbooks Designs for creating a stunning cover.

AUTHOR BIOGRAPHY

When J.J. isn't slumming it with outcasted princes , hunting down sea witches or saving the world from a zombie invasion, you can usually find her nose deep into a book or on adventures with her husband, friends and fur babies.

To keep up with J.J. you can find her on Instagram @author.j.j.marshall or on Facebook in her group Paranormal Depths. If you enjoyed Dark Tides, please leave a review on Amazon or Goodreads.